Six winn...
Six skeletons ...

Plain Jane Kurtz is going to use her winnings to discover her inner vixen. But what's it *really* going to cost her?

New girl in town Nicole Reavis is on a journey to find herself. But what *else* will she discover along the way?

Risk taker Eve Best is on the verge of having everything she's ever wanted. But can she take it?

Young, cocky Zach Haas loves his instant popularity, especially with the women. But can he trust it?

Solid, dependable Cole Crawford is ready to shake things up. But how "shook up" is he prepared to handle?

Wild child Liza Skinner has always just wanted to belong. But how far is she willing to go to get it?

Million Dollar Secrets—do you feel lucky?

Dear Reader,

Have you ever thought about winning the lottery?

Yes? Me, too! Only about a billion times. I've played the "What if I won a million dollars" on many a boring road trip.

One thing that never figures into those dreams—the problems that would arise from that kind of notoriety and that kind of cash. Cole Crawford wasn't expecting those difficulties either. Nor was he expecting the kind of delicious turmoil Jessie Huell would bring into his life.

Cole and Jessie's story was a lot of fun to write. I even played the lottery a time or two to really get the research! Okay, I probably would have played it anyway. That 120 million powerball jackpot is a hard thing to resist. If I win, the pizza will be on me!

I'd love to hear from you. E-mail me at jill@jillmonroebooks.com or visit me on the Web at www.jillmonroe.com.

All my best,

Jill

TALL, DARK AND FILTHY RICH
Jill Monroe

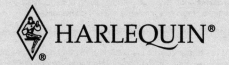

TORONTO • NEW YORK • LONDON
AMSTERDAM • PARIS • SYDNEY • HAMBURG
STOCKHOLM • ATHENS • TOKYO • MILAN • MADRID
PRAGUE • WARSAW • BUDAPEST • AUCKLAND

ISBN-13: 978-0-373-79366-2
ISBN-10:   0-373-79366-9

TALL, DARK AND FILTHY RICH

www.eHarlequin.com

Printed in U.S.A.

ABOUT THE AUTHOR

Jill Monroe makes her home in Oklahoma with her family. When not writing, she spends way too much time on the Internet completing "research" or updating her blog. Even when writing, she's thinking of ways to avoid cooking.

Books by Jill Monroe

HARLEQUIN BLAZE
245—SHARE THE DARKNESS
304—HITTING THE MARK

HARLEQUIN TEMPTATION
1003—NEVER NAUGHTY ENOUGH

Thanks to my husband and family.
I love you and treasure your support.

Special thanks to Gena Showalter—a great dancer
who's taught me all her best moves. Please note
what DOES happen to those who steal garden
gnomes.

Thanks also to Sheila Fields, Donnell Epperson
and Betty Sanders, who always make me laugh
and are always there for me. And to
Kassia Krozser, whose name is always
on my dedication page.

To my friends Jennifer and Karen, who've put up
with a lot during this book. Thanks. I promise to
return to all sweetness and light shortly.

I also want to thank the other authors from the
Million Dollar Secrets books and Kathryn Lye.
It was great fun working with all of you.

1

"EVER THINK MAYBE YOU'RE in the wrong line of work?" Dana, the reporter from the *Atlanta Daily News,* asked in a bored tone as she flipped a Skittle into her mouth.

"No. Why?" Jessica Huell shrugged. So much for the great article the reporter planned to write about Atlanta's Most Interesting Professionals. Clearly, Jessie's execution of her current job was proving to be a dud, and she'd really hoped the exposure from the proffered feature in the newspaper would swing a little more business her way.

Movement caught her eye. "Wait, get down," Jessie said, as she pushed Dana's head below the dashboard.

Both women scrunched low, toward the floorboard of Jessie's car, which was littered with sacks of fast food they'd eaten earlier that night.

Jessie listened. They'd cracked the windows for a little air and to hear the night sounds more easily. At two in the morning, this residential street in Atlanta was quiet. She easily heard the clap of high-heeled shoes on the sidewalk. The opening and closing of a car door. The turning of an engine.

After counting to ten, Jessie poked her head up over the steering wheel. The blue car. *Bingo.* She watched as it drove down the street, then turned left. She counted another ten seconds and then slowly took the same path.

Dana sat up in her seat and rubbed the muscles of her neck. "This wrecks that 'female private investigators are cool' thing I was going for."

Good. Jessie curled her fingers around the steering wheel in satisfaction. Being an investigator could be dangerous and exciting, but when people were drawn to the job for those qualities, that's when folks started getting hurt. Her job entailed hard work, long nights and little sleep. With "boring" thrown in to smooth out the rough edges. A whole lot of boring.

"Whew, I'm glad that's over," Dana said as she rummaged in her purse for something, obviously ready for her one night of undercover to be over. "I don't know how much longer I could stand being in this car."

"Well, we still have a ways to go."

The reporter stopped applying her lip gloss. "Why? You already have the picture of him with the woman."

Jessie dropped back farther from the car she was trailing. Even in a big city like Atlanta, a car closely following another would be suspicious after 2:00 a.m. "A picture tells only part of the story. We don't know who the woman is. What her relationship is to Mr. Roberts."

Dana scoffed. "She hugged him, then stayed in his home for over three hours. I don't think she was the maid. Not with those shoes."

Those were some pretty sexy stilettos. Not that Jessie was much of a shoe person. Not much call for high-heeled sling-backs in her line of work, in spite of the Hollywood image.

Smiling, she kept an eye on the sedan several car lengths ahead. They were back on side streets, where only an occasional streetlight or neon sign broke the darkness. They'd be hitting a residential neighbor-hood soon. She gave a silent plea that the car would lead her to a house with an address rather than to an apartment complex. Those were the worst. A lot of effort wasted on a dead end.

Yes! The owner of the nonmaid shoes was pulling into a paved driveway. Jessie held back, waiting for the woman to enter her home before driving past.

Then she slowly moved forward, looking as casual as she could. Just an insomniatic neighbor out for a drive. Or maybe a desperate mother hoping to get her baby to sleep. Whatever. Blending in. Ap-pearing like someone who belonged there. That was her strength; she'd never been one to stand out. She hated flash, and unlike the reporter beside her, Jessie had never applied lip gloss in a moving vehicle. She wouldn't even know how to take care of a highlight.

With a subtle glance at the number on the front of the house, Jessie was on her way.

"That was a little more fun. It was the closest we've come to getting caught," Dana said, her voice slightly breathless.

"We weren't anywhere near getting caught," Jessie told her dryly. She was all for exaggeration, but not if it made her come across as less than professional.

"No need to get irritated. I just meant it was the first bit of excitement we've had since blondie showed up in the first place. When I still thought this night would be interesting," Dana said with a wink. "What now?"

Dare she tell her? Jessie wondered. Dana was a reporter, after all. The woman dealt with facts. Hopefully.

Actually, Jessie herself should be delving only in facts. Conjecture shouldn't be part of her professional world. But in the lonely hours after midnight, The Speculation Game was often the only thing that kept her awake. And interested. Maybe Dana was right; maybe she needed a different line of work.

Okay, she was losing it. She loved her job. Giving another woman the truth—that the man she was about to marry was a loser—was always good. Or even better, that the man she was about to commit a lifetime to, or at least the next several years to would be "on the level" with her. If only someone had been around to wake up Jessie before her own loser fiancé proved what a louse he was.

She glanced at her companion, whose laptop illuminated the front seat of the car. No, she probably shouldn't tell Dana that on a stakeout she often dabbled in assumptions and bizarre guesses. But then, at nearly three in the morning, common sense was asleep.

"Right about now I start thinking about where she's going."

"What do you mean? We just saw her go into her house." Dana stated, not bothering to look up from her typing.

"No, I mean, what does she plan to do with that stolen microchip he passed along to her?"

Dana stopped typing and gave Jessie an assessing look. "Stolen… I thought he was just some guy who doesn't spend his Thursday nights with his girlfriend."

Jessie put on her best mock-serious expression. "Oh, no. He may come across as a mild-mannered accountant who worked overtime during tax season to buy an engagement ring, but in reality he's escaped from a faraway land. The secret agents from his country have found him."

"The country of Fabricatia, perhaps?" Dana asked, her body language suggesting for the first time this evening that The Speculation Game was something she could get into.

"Exactly. And now he's being stalked by that woman, but determined to keep his secrets safe."

"I knew there was something suspicious about

those pointy-toed sling-backs. Those were total spy shoes. He slipped her a fake chip, I know it."

"But how long can he hold out?"

Dana laughed. "So, do you make up stories like this all evening?"

"Beats the reality of the job."

"No question about that. I was really hoping some irate couple caught in a clandestine tryst might come after you with a gun. Would have made this story a lot more interesting."

"Sorry I couldn't accommodate."

"That was before I knew you. Now I don't want you to get shot at. You can stay with your boring job," Dana said with a smile.

Jessie pulled her car into the parking lot of an all-night diner. "Then you're going to love this next part. You're about to witness the glamorous excitement of plugging this address into the database. Hopefully we'll make a quick hit."

"Ugh. Where's the excitement in that?"

"Did I mention the waffles?"

COLE CRAWFORD FISHED for the package of antacids in his desk, and after ripping open the wrapper, swallowed a few pills without water.

"I caught you," Nicole Reavis said as she poked her head in the doorway.

Cole grimaced. "Yeah, it's already starting out to be one of those days."

"Really? You mean, things aren't working out for the man with a special insight into the minds of women?" she asked with wide-eyed innocence. Fake wide-eyed innocence.

Cole kept his expression neutral. Lately the women in the office had taken to quoting from that fluff piece Dana Roberts had written about him in the *Atlanta Daily News*. Someday he might be able to live down the "sensitive bachelor" line. After a while the receptionist might even stop snickering when delivering mail addressed to "Hottie Producer," as the caption under his picture in the paper had read. Sure, his name was in the piece, but with it buried under phrases like "understands a woman's needs outside of the bedroom" and "has insights into a woman before she even knows them herself," who'd remember?

He regretted ever agreeing to do the interview. Atlanta's Most Interesting Professionals? More like Atlanta's Most Sensitive Pansy-Ass, a profile guaranteed to suck the testosterone right out of his body.

Never again. From now on, he'd leave the spotlight where it belonged—on Eve Best, the star of *Just Between Us*. He'd spotted her talent back when he was stuck producing public-affairs programming for the station. He'd gone with his gut that time. And he'd stick to it from now on.

Nicole waved a newspaper clipping in front of him. "Looks like your favorite reporter has a new victim, and this 'Most Interesting Professional' might make a great segment for the show."

One of Nicole's jobs as a story-segment producer was to scour newspapers, magazines and the Internet for the kind of sex-themed hot topics viewers loved.

Unleashing your Inner Wild Child.

In Praise of Younger Men.

The last few topics on *Just Between Us* had been real winners. Each week brought more viewers. The pressure was mounting to top the previous show. And that was with actual hard work.

Several months ago, he, along with several of his coworkers at the station, had won Georgia's own Lot 'O' Bucks lottery. Thirty-eight million dollars generated a ton of press coverage, and the news division of the station had had a field day with interviews and live feed. So when a former colleague, Liza Skinner, had leaked to the media that she planned to claim part of their winnings, too, things had really gone crazy on the show. With the threat of a lawsuit and the hold up of the money, the advertisers were lining up. New viewers might tune in hoping to catch up on the latest controversy, but stayed because they produced a damn fine show.

With lawyers now involved, their group had opted to shy away from the media. But when one of the winners was Eve Best, star of *Just Between Us,* keeping quiet wasn't always easy. Luckily, the rest of them weren't in front of the camera. Jane Kurtz did the show's makeup. Nicole searched for stories rather than becoming them, and Zach Hass operated the camera.

He still couldn't believe Liza thought she was entitled to any of the money. Sure, she'd given her share into the lottery fund when she worked with them all, but she'd left town without any explanation, and eventually her money had ran out.

Their mistake had been to keep playing her number.

Despite his current appreciation for sodium bicarbonate, Cole thrived on pressure. Which was a good thing. With half the staff taking time off for trips, moving in with one another and weddings, his workload had multiplied. Luckily, things were settling down just in time for the important November ratings period. Sweeps month always took priority over relationships.

He glanced at the newspaper clipping Nicole was now placing on the very large stack of reports, memos and requests already in his in-box. "A private detective?" he asked.

"She's got a bit of an edge. She basically guarantees dirt on anything with a penis."

Ballbusters were great for ratings. He'd book her in spite of becoming a traitor to his gender. "Sounds interesting. You know, you don't need to have me okay your ideas anymore. Feel free to call anyone for an initial Q and A."

"Well, she's from your hometown. I thought you

might know her. According to the article, she's just a few years younger than you."

He'd come from the small town of Thrasher in rural Georgia, and most everyone had stayed in the general area after graduation. Some worked for the many businesses that still thrived there. Others worked on the tree farms, taking care of the tall pines Georgia was so famous for.

He reached for the newspaper clipping and quickly scanned the top paragraph until he found a name. Jessie Huell.

A smile spread across his lips. Sweet little Jessie Huell. Strange profession for someone as soft-hearted as Jessie. But with her father being chief of police, maybe investigation and research were in her blood.

He'd always wondered what had happened to the police chief's good-natured daughter after he'd left. She probably never knew it, but one night she'd saved his life. Did she ever think of him?

He doubted it.

"Do you have a home phone number or just the office one listed here?" he asked.

"Just the office. I figured you'd want to contact her yourself. Plus, with your 'finger on the pulse of women's interests,' I figured you'd have her booked in no time."

And here was the reason for the over-the-counter meds. He tried for stoic.

With a laugh, Nicole quickly left his office. A wise move on her part.

The man with a special insight into the needs of women. Cole scowled. It was enough to make a guy want to shop. For power tools. A good handsaw. Nothing that plugged into the wall. Just something that required plain brute strength.

2

JESSIE ROLLED OUT OF BED and groaned. She flipped off her sleep mask. It was always hard waking up when most people were already several hours into their jobs.

But that wasn't what made her heart start pounding. It was a sense of trouble. The nagging sensation that she'd agreed to…to *something*…wouldn't leave her. After rubbing her eyes, she spotted an envelope by her bedside table, with her handwriting on the back.

Oh, yeah. Phone call. The faint memory of desperately searching for a pen. Writing something down.

Resignation filled her. How many times had she told herself not to answer the phone after being out all night? But with the loss of potential business, she'd never turn her ringer off.

Fully awake now, she could make out the details of the call.

Who the hell had phoned her at the ungodly hour of nine in the morning? Sure, that was probably a normal working time for most people. However, most folks reserved their dirt-worthy behavior for sometime after twilight. Good thing she was a night person.

She stretched, loosening her muscles. The dark panels covering the windows ensured that no bright Atlanta sunshine sneaked into her bedroom while she was trying to sleep.

It had also made finding her ever-moving lamp difficult, until she'd added that clapping device. Great gadget for a fumble-free life. Jessie fluffed one of her pillows, leaned against the padded head-board and took a calm, soothing breath.

From the cloud-soft shades of her pale gold comforter to the harmonious apricot of the drapes, everything about her bedroom was designed to fool her body into sleeping in the middle of the day. Now, if only Jessie could get her phone to cooperate.

She'd probably say yes to anything at nine in the morning, just so she could go back to sleep. She scanned her chicken scratching and prepared herself for what she'd agreed to.

Okay, not too bad. Interview for *Just Between Us*. The Atlanta afternoon talk show she usually watched while eating her breakfast.

Hmm, if this interview worked out, it could be better for business. That profile of her in the newspaper had already provided a nice spike in her income. More weeks like those, and she might be able to pay off the night scope and bullet camera.

Some women bought shoes.

Others liked purses.

Jessie couldn't resist spy gadgets, and she'd been eyeing the Espion Digi-Cam Pen. Illegal in all fifty states, and with a price tag of over two grand, it was enough to make any gal squeal.

She rubbed the muscles of her neck. Sitting in the car always did hellish things to that area of her body. Then she saw the name she'd written underneath the time of her preinterview.

Cole Crawford.

Jessie blamed the fact that she'd fallen into bed way past four for not instantly recognizing it when she'd heard it. She was totally aware now. Her heartbeat quickened and her palms grew moist.

Hell, she was surprised she hadn't written the *O* in the shape of a heart, as she had when she was sixteen. Over and over again in her history notebook she'd also doodled, "Jessie Crawford."

What her sleep-deprived body hadn't experienced this morning, she felt now. Full force. Her mouth went dry. The butterflies in her stomach decided to reemerge.

Maybe it was a good thing Cole Crawford had never kissed her. She probably would have dropped on the spot. Although dropped happy.

He'd been tall and lanky, and her idea of what a boy should look like.

What the hell? Her palms were *tingling,* for crying out loud. His name alone had her reverting to age sixteen. Without even trying. But then, that was always the way. Cole Crawford had never tried anything with her. Not once.

After dropping the envelope on the bed, she stomped into the bathroom and splashed cold water on her heated cheeks. She didn't *want* to see Cole Crawford again. He was her ideal fantasy man, placed high atop his pedestal before she'd realized men could be jerks. He was all that a boy of her dreams should have been. Handsome. Smart. Big shoulders. Why would she ruin it by seeing him now?

Surely what she thought was hot in high school would not be what looked good today. Maybe those "big shoulders" had only appeared muscular and strong, because he was two years older. Maybe he was actually quite scrawny. What if he had grown a unibrow? A mullet? A person could change a lot in nine years.

Stop. Why was she doing this to herself?

Jessie had learned the truth long ago that Santa didn't exist and neither did the tooth fairy. But for some reason she just didn't want to destroy her faith that Cole Crawford was somewhere out there being perfect.

Almost every other illusion she had about life, like soul mates and fidelity, had been stomped into the ground. Couldn't fate allow her to keep this one?

Unfortunately, she'd agreed to a fantasy-snatching appointment when she wasn't thinking straight.

After a quick shower, she padded into her bedroom to peruse her closet. Her wardrobe didn't elicit a lot of "oohs" and "ahhs." She'd never needed much of one to begin with. Until she'd left the force, Jessie had worn her Atlanta PD uniform with pride. Home was casual—jeans and a T-shirt.

Maybe she should have tossed a few bucks toward adding another skirt or shirt in something other than black. But then, black was the only sensible choice on a stakeout.

Wait. There in the back. Something her mother had sent as a desperate attempt to make her girlie. Okay, it was lavender. Not her color of choice, but the blouse was at least professional looking. She paired that with a straight black skirt, her black high-heeled, steel-toed black boots, and her outfit was complete.

What would Cole think of her now?

And why would she care?

After pulling her long, straight blond hair into a ponytail, she brushed out her bangs. Jessie was ready to face the annihilation of her sole remaining castle-in-the-sky, whimsical delusion, which would make Cole Crawford just another guy.

And in case he wasn't, she'd remind herself what kept him off-limits. Cole Crawford was married. With kids.

COLE LEFT HIS OFFICE and walked toward the studio's break room. Jessie Huell should already be in the conference room, but he wanted to buy her a can of Coke before he joined her. He found that he was smiling, anticipating seeing her again.

Maybe they could have a laugh over it. He used to buy her a pop while she conjugated his Latin verbs. His dad had ridden his ass hard back then, and she'd been helping him out. After attending school all day and then working at Mr. Martin's garage all afternoon, he could barely keep his eyes open for homework. Him bringing home a failing grade would have set his old man off.

Cole had probably escaped quite a few smacks due to Jessie's talent with the future perfect tense. Man, at that time, with his day-to-day survival, he couldn't even wrap his brain around the idea of the future. Let alone anything being perfect.

He hadn't allowed himself to think of her. Not in years. What would have been the point? Now, he couldn't wait to see Jessie, to note the changes time had made. Okay, she probably didn't still wear her hair in those long braids, but he doubted her sweet smile had altered.

After buying her Coke, Cole rounded the corner and stopped. His skin grew hot. The bold woman with her back to him, reading one of the *Just Between Us* promo posters, was the kind that should be appreciated. Slowly.

He could spend a lot of time admiring this woman's butt, so nicely packaged in the short black skirt she wore. Or that sexy stretch of skin between where her skirt ended and her boots began.

Did women know just how damn inviting that length of leg was? And those boots…feminine enough to show off an uninhibited sex appeal, but worn with an attitude that said she'd kick the backside of any man stupid enough to act like a jerk.

His kind of woman. A million carnal fantasies flashed in his mind.

He swallowed, feeling good. This was the first time in a long time he'd responded so physically to someone. But who was she?

The chill of the cold aluminum can finally jerked him back to reality. He needed to find Jessie. Cole looked down the hallway to see if maybe she'd wandered off. She was always curious. It was a trait that often got her into trouble. And had once saved his skin.

Then the woman turned and he forgot the cold.

Cole had been right. He'd never fail to recognize Jessie's smile. It was still the same, but everything else had changed. She'd grown a little taller, and those shapely legs of hers invited serious appreciation. Her breasts, round and full, drew a man's eyes. And that mouth, sensual and carnal, promised a lot of wicked things. The woman in front of him could never be called sweet.

Her brown eyes tipped up in the corners with her widening smile. She knew. She knew she'd surprised him, and what's more, he knew she liked it.

"Hello, Cole. It's been a while."

"Little Jessie Huell," he said, his voice filled with wonder.

She was beautiful. Her lips twisted and she raised an eyebrow. "Not so little anymore."

As if he needed to be reminded. For some reason, he thought that if he called her little, he might see her as that. Idiot. Was it really Jessie Huell's mouth he'd just imagined on his own?

She walked toward him slowly. Every step reminding him how long it was since he'd been attracted to someone. A year and a half. A year and a half since his wife had left.

"I bought you a Coke." The gesture seemed lame now. Men didn't bring this woman soft drinks. They brought her jewelry.

A soft smile touched her lips. "Like when we studied Latin?"

He nodded as the scent of her ambushed him. She smelled like sunshine, and he was transported back to a time when his whole life had stretched golden before him. A time when the mistakes you made were on geometry tests and missed free throws, not with your life.

"De oppresso liber," she murmured, as her fingers wrapped around the can.

The phrase meant "Free from having been oppressed." Once, he'd been leaving the garage for their Latin study session. He'd kept her waiting for over forty minutes. She'd gasped when he stretched out in the booth across from her, sporting the beginnings of a black eye. He hadn't gotten out of his father's way fast enough that time.

She hadn't said a thing. Simply wrote the phrase on his notebook. Then below that, she'd written *Someday* in English. Someday. She didn't know it, but he'd held on to that bit of encouragement with everything he had. Sometimes it was *all* he had.

Together, they'd sipped their Cokes in silence. The sun had set, and the crickets started to chirp. With his eye nearly swollen shut, he hadn't needed another thing but Jessie's quiet understanding.

That memory told him how dangerous his attraction for her would be. Because he couldn't need anything. Too many needed *him* already. A pair of little girls depended on him to make the right decisions.

He dropped his hand from the soda, took a step away from the teasing scent that beckoned to him, and closed his mind to the past. He could do without having his emotions stripped bare right now.

Jessie popped the top of the can and took a sip. "I've switched to diet, but every now and then I miss the taste of Coke with sugar. Of course, you probably hear this kind of talk from all the women in the office and your wife."

"I'm not married."

She looked up at him sharply.

It was the first time Jessie's smile slipped.

3

THE ONE THING that had been holding her back from making a complete idiot of herself over seeing him was now gone.

Cole Crawford wasn't married.

Damn, she really *should* have paid more attention to her mother's newsy e-mails about her hometown. That might have prevented the shakiness she felt right now.

Turning, she took a large swallow of pop. The sweet drink gave her body an instant jolt.

Who was she kidding? Cole gave her that jolt. She'd crushed on him big-time. But he'd gone off to college, found someone new and gotten married. Jessie had forced all her feelings for him into a hidden corner of her mind and locked them there.

Now that lock was open and hope was chasing away the shadows. She was suddenly having all kinds of amazing fantasies. Okay, she was playing something far more dangerous than The Speculation Game; instead, she was sporting around in Exaggeration Land. Grrr.

Cole followed her into the conference room, then pulled out one of the chairs at the long table, offering her a seat. At least she could give her weakened knees a break.

Jesse tried to smile politely rather than glare at him. He was supposed to be in some far-off, remote place, being untouchable and gorgeous.

He wasn't supposed to be right here in Atlanta, being single and a buffet of lick-me kiss-me carnality. If he *had* to be somewhere near her, he could have at least been sporting a large, protruding gut over those khakis.

She'd bet Cole's abs would make any male model run home and cry for his mommy.

Dammit.

She took a measured breath. Yes, she was being ridiculous. She was a mature woman who'd built a business from the ground up. And she was here to discuss that business. "Did you want to ask me a few questions?" she said, thrilled that her voice sounded so unaffected.

His eyes narrowed, then he seemed to notice the notebook in his hand, and gave a chagrinned shrug. "I was just getting over the grown-up you. I was expecting braids."

"I hope I wouldn't still be wearing the Laura Ingalls look at my age," she said, as she watched him slide into the chair opposite from her.

"So tell me about your job," he began, after giving her legs one last look. "You're a P.I.?"

"I dig up dirt."

He raised an eyebrow questioningly. "What if you can't find any?"

Why did people never believe? All the naiveté… Sometimes it made her a little sad. But it was good for business. "Everyone has dirt. Some you sweep under a rug and forget about. Some you bury alive."

His hazel eyes challenged her. "Think you could dig up any dirt on me?" he asked, his voice lower. More sensual.

She stopped herself from sucking in a breath. While some girls went for the cute boys, the tall basketball players or the preppy charmers, Jessie had always been a sucker for the guys who liked fast cars. The rebels without a cause. Yeah, fast and dangerous. That was all Cole Crawford.

He may have smoothed out the edges, but underneath, she sensed the danger still lurked.

And she still went for it.

Her agency had been created to protect women just like her. Those who liked a man with a bit of an edge. Would she find dirt on this man? She could guarantee it.

"I bet I could have a juicy bit on you in less than thirty seconds," she told him with a laugh. Her body liking the idea of the challenge.

The hazel of his eyes darkened to brown. She'd

forgotten about his beautiful eyes—sometimes green, sometimes brown, depending on his thoughts.

Mmm, no, she hadn't forgotten; she'd just wanted to.

Any woman would take a moment and bask in the sheer pleasure of his gaze. Savor it like some delicious dessert. Chocolate and Cole's eyes. Two things a gal could never get enough of.

His knee accidentally brushed hers as he shifted in his chair. Sensation raced down her leg, and she stared at him. There was plenty of space between them. There was no reason for him to *accidentally* touch her.

Wait a minute. Was Cole Crawford flirting with her? She wasn't looking for it, had never expected it, so it would come as a bit of a shock…but the signs were all there.

The way he'd angled his big, broad shoulders toward her to totally focus on what she had to say, as if he planned to do nothing but listen.

Or how his gorgeous eyes held her gaze just a moment longer than necessary. Then there was the teasing about finding dirt on him.

Cole had teased her when they were in high school, but it hadn't been like *that*. Sensual. His voice had never lowered, his glance never flicked to her lips as his playful actions elicited shivers down her back.

"Oh, I'm sure you could find something."

Her nipples hardened. He'd accepted the challenge.

A young woman, who looked fresh out of college, knocked on the open door of the conference room.

He reluctantly looked away from Jessie. "What's up, Penny?"

"Bad news. Nicole wanted me to let you know our guest for today's show just bailed. So should we do another Eve chat?"

"Eve chat?" Jessie asked.

"That's when Eve walks into the audience and they ask questions and chat," Penny explained.

"You're kidding! That's what you do when someone doesn't show up? I figured those shows were only aired on Fridays."

"We also work them into the schedule when this comes up. You never know when a guest will cancel at the last minute."

Jessie sat back in her chair. "Wow, you'd never guess that. Eve seems so natural."

"That's why she's so good at her job," Cole told her.

"So, what do you want me to tell Nicole? Go with the Eve chat?"

Cole glanced Jessie's way, and her shoulders suddenly tensed. She knew by the change in his expression, the speculation that entered his hazel eyes, that he was contemplating asking her to fill in. Being on TV seemed like a great idea, but at such short notice? And on only a few hours' sleep?

Contemplating the purchase of a vehicle GPS

location tracker when the new money started rolling in was all fun and games until the reality of appearing on TV hit her. She could look a total fool. She could babble. She could freeze. Something could be hanging from her nose and she wouldn't know, but everyone else in Atlanta would have seen it. Who would hire a P.I. who had stuff coming out of her nose?

Jessie took a deep breath. She grabbed the Coke can and swallowed a large mouthful of pop.

"You up for being our guest today?" Cole asked. His eyes held a daredevil challenge.

No. "Sure," she said with a forced shrug. She wanted this. Her business *needed* this. She had never backed down from anything in her life, and she wasn't going to start now. She'd just make certain she looked in a mirror before stepping in front of a camera.

Jessie straightened her shoulders and placed the Coke can on the conference table with resolve. Sure, being in a situation where she could humiliate herself and have it remembered for years to come, not to mention bring shame to the Huell family name, was a possibility...so why would she want to turn that down?

"I'll tell Nicole," Penny gushed.

Jessie turned toward Cole. "I'm looking forward to it."

A slow, sexy smile spread across his face. "Thought I might have lost you for a minute there," he said.

Hmm. She was usually pretty good at schooling

her features. In fact, she was proud of her ability to hide from people what she was thinking. And feeling. Was she slipping?

Or maybe Cole could read people a lot better than she'd given him credit for. She'd have to remember that.

"I'll take you over to makeup."

Cole stood and escorted her down the hall. He'd grown taller since the last time they'd walked side by side. His shoulders were broader, too.

So many things had changed since he was her high-school fantasy.

Lines fanned from his eyes, indicating he still liked to laugh. But deep grooves circled his lips, proving he'd experienced some of life's harder times. And what had happened to his wife?

With no other obstacles in their way…

Would this be Jessie's chance?

Her chance to finally touch him, kiss him, be with Cole the way she'd wanted to since she'd first seen him on that loud, rusty motorcycle her dad had hated so much.

No. No, for some reason she liked her fantasy and wanted to keep it intact. Knowing Cole's true flaws would be a letdown. And every gal needed at least one unattainable dream to make life interesting.

"Do I have time to run home and change? I wasn't expecting to be on the air today."

His gaze scanned her body. Her skin heated as it

moved from her face, down her neck, to linger on her chest. Her nipples began to bud and her stomach tightened as his eyes moved lower. And lower.

All the green was gone from the hazel when his eyes met hers once more, betraying a raw desire. "You don't need to change," he said, his voice low again and husky. With a nod, he indicated the door marked Makeup, then he turned and left.

Jessie leaned against the wall as she recovered from her body's reaction to the lust in his eyes. The fast heartbeat, hitch in her breath, the perspiration…they were all there. And suddenly she realized she was wrong.

Maybe knowing the real Cole would be more than enough. More than enough to give up on her fantasy man. With a smile, she headed into the makeup room.

Fifteen minutes later, she was sitting in the make-up artist's chair, trying to hold her tongue. It was hard. Jane's nonstop talk about her new boyfriend had put Jessie at ease, but it took everything she had not to blurt out her typical warnings. "You hooked up in Vegas?" "How easily can you replace that wall between your two condos?"

Ordinarily, Jessie wouldn't have anything in common with the fashionable blonde, but Jane was obviously so happy and made her feel so comfortable, she couldn't help but like her right away. But Jessie hated to see anyone's heart stomped on, so she thought maybe just one small word of caution about men would be in order.

She'd have to break her in easy. Maybe start with a quick suggestion of a simple Google search before she moved on to credit checks and criminal background reports. "Do you have a computer at home?"

With a flick of her wrist, Jane spun the chair so Jessie could finally see herself in the mirror.

And she forgot all about tips on securing a man's social-security number. "Wow." She moved her head from side to side. "I have cheekbones."

Jane laughed. As if she had this kind of response to her abilities every day, but still loved it.

"You make me look like this all the time, and I'll check out that new man of yours for free."

"No, I'm not worried." A smile so peaceful passed across her face that Jessie's inborn worries grew. Only a woman who truly loved would have a smile like that, and was therefore more likely to ignore her man's faults.

"Besides, I can show you how to look like that in ten minutes," Jane said as she put away a few of her brushes. "Makeup is the easy part. Unleashing your inner wild child, now, that's…"

Her words trailed off, and Jessie got the impression the woman was reliving some delicious memory.

"Come on, I'll take you to the green room."

"When will I meet Eve?" she asked as she followed Jane to the door.

"Normally you would have already, but since you're a last-minute fill-in, probably not until just before showtime. Sometimes Eve likes it that way, to keep things fresh."

They passed by open double doors to a large studio, and Jessie stopped. Audience members were already filing into their seats. A charged energy positively radiated from the room. The leather furniture of the interview area, which seemed to fill up her TV screen at home, appeared miniature now against the backdrop of lights, cameras and the half-dozen or so crew members milling around the studio floor.

Getting tickets to *Just Between Us* was the new hot thing. Atlantans waited in line excitedly for hours. Now they were going to see *her.* And be utterly disappointed.

Jessie sucked in a breath. Her skin grew clammy and her nerves started fluttering.

"You'll do great," said a deep voice she recognized.

Cole had returned, and was in the process of placing a reassuring hand on her shoulder. Except the touch that was supposed to be comforting was anything but. Once again her nipples tightened beneath the lavender material of her awful blouse.

She turned, and Cole's eyes widened. His expression grew more serious. Jessie had forgotten Jane's ministrations to her face. "How do you like the new me?" she asked, shooting for glib.

"Nice. I liked the old you, too," he said, his voice deep, his eyes intent.

Those butterflies inside her tummy disappeared as her stomach clenched in reaction to his words. Because Cole wasn't just saying he liked how that kid he'd known from the past had matured, he was acknowledging the new attraction between them.

A surge of strength made her muscles loosen. This was something she could handle. Wanted to handle. Desire…passion.

"I have your microphone. It's wireless, so you won't have to remove your shirt." He held the small device up for her to see. "Ready?" he asked.

Maybe. She worked to make her breathing normal when she felt his warm fingers brush the swell of her breast. The scent of him wafted toward her…citrus, with just a hint of mint. She struggled not to wiggle as he clipped the microphone in place.

How long did this take?

"You look hot, Jessie." They both turned to see Penny walking toward them. "Nicole wanted me to wait with Jessie in the green room until her segment," she told Cole.

He nodded. "That's fine." Clearly, the young woman was in awe of him. Who wouldn't be, with the sense of power that hung around him? At the same time, there was something about authority that made Jessie want to challenge it.

Not a great quality to have when working as a police officer.

A must-have for a P.I.

Cole's hazel eyes cut back to her. "Break a leg," he said with a slow wink.

She watched him walk away, and Jessie vowed she would never watch this man walk away from her again, until she knew the secret delights those eyes of his promised.

FITTING HER FOR THE microphone had been a bad move. Penny could have done it. Hell, twelve other people on staff could have managed it. Feeling the softness of Jessie's skin had teased him, but spotting the hint of her sexy, black lace bra foretold his doom. He hadn't been able to concentrate since the show began taping. Thankfully, the director had the action well in hand.

All Cole had to do was sit in the control booth and speculate on the black skirt she wore. Would it ride up? That expanse of skin between skirt and boot had teased him before, in the conference room. Now, it tortured him, because he knew just how soft her skin was. Would the inside of her thighs be as delicate? His fingers curled into a fist.

The stagehands finished the change to the set from the last segment, and Eve and Jessie took their seats on stage.

The director flipped on his studio mic. "Cue music, we're back in five, four, three…"

As the music faded, Eve took over with a smile. "We're here with Jessie Huell, who's been sharing some of her stories of late-night chases pursuing cheating spouses. So, Jessie, give some advice for the single girls out there. What should we be on the lookout for?"

"Take camera two," the director said, and the monitor filled with a close-up shot of Jessie's beautiful face.

She laughed, a deep feminine sound, yet filled with cynicism. That was it. Cole hadn't been able to place what was different about the sweet, innocent girl he'd known. Suspicion, skepticism surrounded her now.

"First of all, you need to be prepared that he's holding something back. News you might not want to hear or know."

"Camera one, go to a two-shot," announced the director.

"How can you be sure of that?"

"Because everyone's got a secret. In fact, you show me a man who's lived in the world, had a job, gone to college or whatever, who *doesn't* have at least one thing he wouldn't want you to know, and I'll show you a man who's a liar. Or someone who's very good at covering his tracks. And that's just what I like to do…uncover tracks."

"How do you go about it?"

"Camera three, pan the crowd for audience reaction."

"Other than the background searches, you have to

become an investigator and think systematically. Find out what your target's hidden objective is. We all have one. Certainly every man I've encountered has. Maybe it is to find love, his soul mate. Maybe it's to get to something you have."

Cole scanned the audience's reaction. Jessie held their attention. Good.

"Here's the second step. Find out the reason behind your man's actions. What's he trying to hide? Some dirt you can live with, some dirt you can't. Why is he with you instead of some other woman? Ask yourself that before you enter into any kind of relationship. Is he cheating? Using you? Be methodical and be brutal. And remind yourself that love has nothing to do with it."

"So what does that leave a woman with?" Eve asked. Damn, she was good. Cole had been wondering the same thing.

"Back to camera two."

A sexy smile tugged at the corner of Jessie's lips. "Now, that's where the beauty of the fling comes in. I highly recommend it. But like your investigation, you have to be systematic about it. There are rules."

"This I've got to hear."

"Get rid of anything casual. No quick phone calls just to talk. The telephone should only be used to set up times for sex."

Cole's penis hardened.

"Second, don't sleep over. You're not twelve."

"Got it," Eve said.

"Never engage your emotions, and last, but certainly not least, don't ever let him see how much you want him."

"Terrific. Thanks, Jessie."

"Wind down and cue music. Close segment in five, four…"

Eve grinned into the camera. "There you have the rules for your next fling. We all have secrets, and it's Jessie Huell's job to discover what they are. Join us after the break."

"And to commercial," the director said, and took off his headset. "You found a good one there, Cole. I bet our viewers will be contemplating their boyfriend's covert objectives, or their spouse's hidden intentions for weeks."

The smile left Cole's face. He forced the speculation about Jessie's cynicism from his mind. She was in the habit of finding dirt, and he was a man who'd lived in the world of sandstorms. Yes, she was intriguing. But she was also a woman of secrets. And most secrets were best left alone.

4

HAD SHE REALLY ANNOUNCED to the world she believed only in flings?

Jessie closed her eyes for a moment and sighed. That fling comment should definitely make her mother proud. Jessie could picture the scene at the Cuts and Such salon, where her mom never failed to get her hair back-combed every Saturday. Her mother would be innocently thumbing through a magazine under the dryer, when she'd be bombarded by the tsk-tsk-tsks of her friends. Each commiserating that she'd never make grandparent status with that kind of daughter.

But the fling observation wasn't the best part of the ill-fated interview. Jessie had quickly followed her statement about flings by announcing—most emphatically—that all men were basically big lying liars.

That pretty much ensured no dates in the foreseeable future. She'd almost shouted that any man who asked her out would be practically finger-printed. If she'd learned one thing in her line of work, it was that guys liked their secrets kept hidden.

Oh, well. It's not as if anyone had been wearing

a path in the grass to get to her, anyway. Plus, she'd have no time for dating, because her client list was sure to expand. After the show, she'd taken a cue from Eve and spent the next twenty minutes talking with audience members. Jessie had almost run out of business cards. That alone would be worth any embarrassment associated with appearing on *Just Between Us.*

Crew members, from the camera operator to assistant producers, congratulated her on her performance. When the receptionist handed her three pink message slips asking for return calls, the last of any I-said-too-much qualms vanished.

"That went great," Penny told her, as she took off Jessie's microphone before dashing away to do something else.

Jane came by with a small white box. "These facial wipes will take off the makeup if you want."

Jessie shook her head, her blond hair flowing around her shoulders. Pretty different from her normal ponytail. "I think I'll keep it on. Makes me feel a bit glamorous, and I can't remember the last time I wore makeup."

"Not even on a date?"

"Who's dating, with my upside-down schedule? I'm hitting work at the time most people are heading to bed."

Eve approached them. Jessie had always thought the woman was charismatic on TV, but in person she was stunning. "That was a great interview, Jessie," she said.

Jessie immediately felt her sincerity. "Really? I was afraid I was coming off a little cynical."

Eve shook her head. "The studio audience was loving it. I could have used you myself in the past. I've had a boyfriend or two who I know had a lot of dirt. Speaking of which, I heard you went to high school with Cole. Now, that's some dirt I want to hear."

"You knew Cole in school?" Penny asked as she returned to Jessie's side. "Was he hot then, too?" She giggled.

Yes.

Jessie resisted the urge to say, "Hey, that wasn't so long ago," complete with a giggle of her own. Then she realized Eve and Jane were also looking at her expectantly. Her eyes narrowed as she glanced from one woman to the other. Now this was interesting. These ladies were really curious about Cole, which meant that he likely hadn't changed much from the keep-everything-to-himself teen he'd been. And just like always, women wanted to know his secrets.

Jessie did know some of them. They were some of hers, too. But although she was in the business of spilling other people's secrets, she kept hers under lock and key. "Uh…"

"Uh-oh. I can see we've made you uncomfortable," Penny said. Then her face brightened. "Hey, you should go out with us tonight for our end-of-the-week stress down. Cole will be there."

"End of the week? But it's Thursday," Jessie said, feeling confused.

"Right after the sign-off for the Friday show, Cole leaves town and heads over to his sister's place to see his daughters."

"So really, Thursday is our Friday," Penny told her.

Jane nodded. "And that's why Fridays are our worst shows."

Eve shrugged. "Or our best. Depends, really."

Both Eve and Jane laughed. Clearly this was an inside joke. But Jessie was getting really good information about Cole. Excellent. Now she had an explanation about where his kids were, and she'd avoided having to look through filed court cases. Those were the worst. If she had enough money— Wait a minute! *When.* When she had enough money to hire an assistant, poking through judgments would be the first thing reassigned.

Man, this was almost too easy. Jessie hadn't even had to resort to the tools of the trade. Blank expression. Innocent-sounding questions. Where was the challenge?

Just then Cole came striding toward their group, looking far more relaxed than earlier, but still very, very sexy.

Hmm. Here was her challenge now. A little thrill

ran down Jessie's back. Little? Who was she kidding? Her whole body grew tingly. It was ready to take up the task at hand. Cole.

"Tell him you want to go to Club Octane," Eve said, her lips twisting as if she were trying to hide a grin.

Jessie glanced toward him. She sucked in a quick breath, because the purposeful way he was moving in her direction reminded her of a dark gym when she was fifteen. High-school dance.

Oh, the agony and the angst of not being asked to dance. She'd spent thirty minutes with her back against the padded gym wall, the basketball net casting a shadow across her face. She'd stood there, feeling miserable and asking herself the same thing over and over again: why had she come?

As others danced and moved about on the gym floor, she'd sometimes spotted Cole. Her face would flush and her breath would hitch, reminding her why'd she been idiot enough to attend this dance.

Then Cole had walked toward her.

He'd asked her to dance. With a nod, she'd joined him on the floor, her heart beating so loudly it overpowered the music. The song pounding from the speakers changed to something slow and seductive, and Cole drew her closer. She took a deep breath. Memorized the smell of him. He'd worn cologne that night. It reminded her of the woods, but didn't mask the scents she associated with him. Leather from his jacket. Or the harsh soap he used to clean his greasy hands after working in the garage.

She'd closed her eyes as she settled her forehead on his chest. Jessie vowed she'd dance this one song and leave. She knew this was a pity dance. Cole was trying to save her from the embarrassment of not having been asked out onto the floor even once. But she didn't care. She would have taken Cole any way she could have got him.

Cole Crawford had tried to save her back then. As he was doing now, by infiltrating this gang of female coworkers and helping to pull her out of a potentially awkward situation. How sweet. But Jessie was more than capable of saving herself. In fact, Cole should be concerned about saving *himself*. From her.

She flashed him a smile, and his steps slowed for half a beat. She made sure her lips didn't turn up in satisfaction. Cole might not be so immune to her as he'd been in high school. "Your colleagues were inviting me to join you for your Thursday night out. Club Octane good for you?"

Cole shuddered. Ah, the ladies were setting her up to make him uncomfortable, Jessie realized. Excellent. She'd play along. "So what's wrong with Club Octane?"

"Two words. 'Dancing Queen.'"

Eve and Jane laughed, but Jessie was still confused. "I don't get it."

"The probability of me having to dance to an

ABBA song is perilously high at Octane. I've never met a woman who wouldn't dance to that song, and try to drag me onto the floor with her. Not going to happen."

Eve draped her arm around Cole's shoulders. "You see, according to the *Atlanta Daily News,* Cole here has his finger on the pulse of what women want. So like any man…he's not going to give it to them. No dancing."

Jane shook her head sadly. "Ever since that article came out, it's been only sports bars."

Cole raised an eyebrow. "It hasn't been all bad for you."

She nodded. "True, I actually participated in the fantasy-sports league. Won an HDTV Big Screen with surround sound."

"You never saw so many grown men crying in their beer," Cole said dryly.

Jessie laughed. She loved it. The camaraderie. The teasing. She'd missed that since she'd left the force. Hadn't even realized she had until now. Maybe that was because—

Stop. She wasn't going to do this. She wasn't searching for inner reasons.

"I'm going to call Perry and see if he wants to join us at Latitude 33. I'll meet you there," Jane said with a wave.

"Good idea. I'll call Mitchell, and invite Nicole."

And that left Jessie and Cole alone together.

"Perry and Jane live together, and Mitchell is Eve's boyfriend," Cole told her.

"Ah," Jessie said with a nod.

The smile faded from his eyes as Cole faced her. "Thanks, Jessie. You really came through for us today. But then you always come through, don't you?"

The light atmosphere disappeared instantly. Jessie's jaw almost dropped. Could he actually be referring to that fateful night that nearly killed him and sent her to her father for help? Here? In the impersonal beige hallways of some TV station?

No, she was inferring way too much. Jessie gave a light laugh, wanting to lighten the mood. "Yes, well, I can see all that Latin Ablative Absolute work we did has really paid off in the work force."

Cole's eyes crinkled in the corners as he smiled. "I don't even remember what that is."

"I just remember it was hard." Did she want to steer the conversation back to the questions she always wanted to ask? No, she could enjoy her visit down memory lane to a point, but there were memories she didn't want to relive. Cole leaving her without a word was one of them.

No, better to keep it light. She glanced at the banks of TV monitors. All on different channels. It felt surreal. Uncomfortable. Jessie nodded her head toward the row of screens. "It's strange, but I feel I'm being watched."

"It's a TV station. You can't escape it. But I know

what you mean. If you're ready, I'll walk you to the restaurant. It's only a block from the studio."

That was the nice thing about the midtown area of Atlanta. Places to eat, shop, live and work were all within easy walking distance.

Cole led her to the reception area. With a wave to the security guard chatting to the receptionist, they emerged onto the sidewalk. Jessie blinked as the late afternoon sun hit her eyes, and she rummaged in her purse for sunglasses. With her odd schedule, she'd become a creature of the night, and bright sunlight really bothered her.

The click of her boot heels on the pavement was the only sound for a while. The weather was still mild for this time of year in Georgia, and Jessie took a moment to enjoy it—the warmth of her skin, the sun on her hair. Days like this were few and far between.

Cole reached for her hand and drew her into the shade and out of the way of foot traffic. He'd donned his own sunglasses, but the set of his lips was stern.

"I know you were cornered in there. You don't have to go. I'll call Eve's cell right now and—"

Jessie placed a hand on his arm, feeling the muscles tighten beneath her fingertips. "No, it's okay. I think it will be a lot of fun."

His expression grew dubious. "You realize they are going to grill you."

She pushed her sunglasses to the top of her head

and gave him a wink. "Actually, I promised them a lot of dirt. Yours."

His shoulders stiffened. "Then maybe we should talk about this. There are…*events* I don't discuss with any…"

As his words trailed off, the tension ramped up between them. Jessie swallowed. Hard. She knew exactly what things, what events Cole was referring to.

She returned her hand to Cole's arm. "It's okay. I'm not going to talk about *events.*" She'd be thrilled to never think about what had happened that night. Ever. "Some stories are best left in the past," she said, hoping her voice was reassuring.

His eyes met hers. Searched hers. Jessie forced out a laugh, trying to lighten the mood. "Besides, those ladies want the kind of dirt they can tease you about. Something embarrassing from high school. Like falling out of your seat in second period or getting caught passing notes in class. Maybe I should tell them you actually wore pajamas on pajama school spirit day." Which had never happened.

His shoulders relaxed and his upper lip lifted in a half smile. "I don't think they'd believe you."

"I don't think they would, either."

The heat of his gaze faded, and his eyes turned hazel once more. He shifted his shoulders, and his body language became neutral. The barrier had returned. There was a detachment about Cole. There always had been. Oh, he was more at ease around people now, his "hands off" attitude more toned down. But it still lingered. That was probably why the women in his office took so much pleasure in teasing him. That article gave them the right tool to find a chink in his heavy emotional armor.

Jessie didn't like barriers. Not anymore. They could hurt people. Her line of work was all about breaking barriers down. Discovering why someone needed those barricades. She didn't like this newest wall Cole had just planted between the two of them. "Where can I get a copy of that article everyone was talking about?"

Cole turned and drew her back onto the sidewalk. "Forget it," he said.

She tugged her sunglasses onto her nose and cautioned herself that the warm hand at the small of her back was some alpha male show of courtesy.

"You might as well give it to me. I'm a private detective, after all. I have my ways, you know."

"You'll just have to use them. I'm not about to make this easy for you."

She wouldn't want it any other way.

He led her to a building with a large sign proclaiming Latitude 33. Before Cole could even open the door, Jessie heard the low roar that could only be a crowd enjoying happy hour. She stepped inside. Yes, definitely a sports bar. Rows of televisions playing football, soccer, baseball and golf littered the place. Decorations representing every conceivable sport hung from the ceiling, draped over doorways and lined the walls. From the back of the room she heard the break of pool balls on one of the six green-felt-covered tables.

And the tempting smell of nachos. Her mouth watered.

Someone tapped her on the shoulder and she turned to find Eve. "So, what do you think?" she asked.

"Wow. It's like man heaven."

"You haven't even seen the upstairs. That's where they have the interactive games. You can try your hand at golf or the batting cages. Nothing like slamming a ball into the wall to relieve a little stress. It's actually a lot of fun."

"Just don't let that secret out on your show or men might start thinking sports bars are the perfect setting for proposals, birthdays and anniversaries."

"Good point. Ah, there's Nicole. She was finding us a table. I'll introduce you to everyone else. And they can't wait to meet you." Eve glanced toward Cole with a playful smile. "We're having a bet on who can get the best story from you about Cole."

He rolled his eyes, but took the ribbing good-naturedly.

"You should be worried," Jessie warned him. "I can be bought. Maybe you giving me that article doesn't sound half-bad now. You know I can do some damage to you."

JESSIE WAS RIGHT. She *could* do a lot of damage to him. Ever since the word *fling* had come from her beautiful mouth, he'd been trying not to picture her naked. Although that was just an excuse. He'd been picturing her naked since he'd spied those sexy legs of hers in the conference room.

This was not the awkward, innocent girl from his past. This was a woman who was smart, knew what she wanted and didn't make a man look twice at her, because no man would be fool enough to take his eyes off her in the first place.

This evening had become sweet agony. Sweet because she fitted into his network of colleagues and friends so easily. Over the past hour they'd laughed, ate and generally enjoyed each other's company. Agony, because he couldn't get his mind off the potential softness of her lips. Or that spark of sexy mischief in her dark brown eyes. Or how she shifted in her seat, providing him a new, painful glimpse of her thigh. It should be illegal for this woman to wear short skirts.

In public, he amended. With him, in private, she could wear or not wear whatever she damn well wanted to.

He watched as Eve laughed about something Jessie had said. Jessie drew him. Looking back now, he realized she probably always had. Any number of people could have helped him with his Latin. Any number of people weren't the police chief's daughter, and yet still, he'd needed her company. He'd been attracted to her openness and giving spirit before. Jessie had always reminded him of sunshine.

But now...

Now the hints of what could happen in the darkness joined her sunny promise. Suddenly he wanted her more than he'd wanted anything in a long, long time. And it was futile. Like the tense of those Latin verbs she used to help him with, everything about this situation was imperfect. The past was the past. He'd been an idiot to bring it into the present.

Anyway, it didn't matter, because he had to get out of there. A new hell was starting in the bar. Karaoke.

5

THERE WERE TWO THINGS Jessie did really, really poorly in a bar. She couldn't tie a cherry stem with her tongue and she couldn't sing karaoke. Why she was expected to do either one, she didn't know. The first, she probably wouldn't have to attempt today. The second, well, "The Love Shack" was playing, and Penny wanted to hop on the stage and drag Jessie along with her.

"I'd pay cash money to see Eve up there," Cole said.

"You'd need a lot," Eve told him.

He laughed. "I just happen to have a winning lottery ticket."

"Which right now isn't worth the paper it's printed on. And it *still* wouldn't be enough."

"You guys are so boring. I'm going to request 'These Boots Are Made for Walking.' Jessie, you'll sing with me, won't you?" Penny asked.

"She just agreed to play darts with me," Cole said, standing.

Jessie turned her head and mouthed "thank you" to him, because her singing voice could clear the room. Cole offered his hand and helped her to her feet. His fingers wrapped around hers.

To be honest, Jessie had always expected to feel some cheesy clichéd sensation, such as a zap of electricity, if he ever held her hand. She was right. It was cheese on top of cheese, because her whole body experienced a high voltage shock thanks to this man's touch. She wanted to pull away quickly or hang on tighter all at the same time.

She tried to gauge from his expression if he'd felt the same thing, but he was already leading her through the bar to the game section.

Upstairs, the lighting was low, allowing the LED displays on the various games to glow brightly. What would they do? What would they talk about? She was reminded of those times she'd wait for him at the diner. The sole dating advice her mother had ever offered consisted of the woman's responsibility to keep the conversation flowing. Jessie had been filled with nervous anticipation.

Now she was just curious. Curious about Cole. About his divorce that no one back home seemed to know about. Which probably wasn't surprising since he had no family left in their hometown of Thrasher.

As a young girl she'd wondered how his lips would feel against hers. As a woman, she wondered what kind of lover he'd be. How he'd use his hands. Stroke or caress? What his skin would feel like beneath her own fingertips. Whether he'd be quick to get—

"Steel-tipped or soft?" he asked.

She blinked at him. "Excuse me?"

He nodded toward the darts. Good thing the lights were low in here, because she felt an embarrassed blush on her cheeks. She'd gotten a bit carried away with her thoughts.

She could play this off. No problem. "What's the difference?" she asked, her voice growing husky.

"Soft is best if you're not as experienced. No one gets hurt with a wild throw. The steel-tipped darts are harder and penetrate the board easier, but are a lot more dangerous."

Jessie swallowed. Harder. Penetrate. Oh, my. "Maybe we should stick with the soft." And maybe she should get a grip. What was wrong with her? This was darts. In a bar, for crying out loud. Not everything had to remind her of sex.

He handed her a dart and she smiled in thanks. She gave a quick practice toss, then fired. Missing her target by a mile.

Cole laughed. "You're really bad at this."

Jessie laughed with him. "You know what makes it worse? As a P.I., I have a license to carry a gun."

He groaned.

"Okay, in all fairness, I think the last time I played darts it involved Velcro and I was nine. I'm actually a good shot with a rifle or handgun."

"I might have to see that to believe it." He reached for her hand, giving her another dart, and she experienced another jolt. "See those grooves along the shaft? That's where you want to wrap your fingers. Hold firmly. Try to use your whole hand around the shaft. The more area your fingers touch, the better your control."

And maybe she should just call "time" and go with the fact that this sounded like hand-job instructions. Or that she might not mind brushing up on her technique with Cole.

Then he wrapped his arm around her, enveloped her in his heat. "Pull back, aim. Release."

Her dart sailed through the air.

"Bull's-eye," he said, his lips just above her ear. His breath a caress.

Never again would she look at darts as anything other than foreplay. She glanced upward, and their eyes met. His gaze dropped to her mouth, and she felt her nipples harden. Her lips parted.

Cole dropped his arm. "Here," he said, handing her another dart. "Try again."

He didn't put his arm around her after that, but the atmosphere between them had changed. Intensified.

After playing a full round, they made their way back to the others. Cole didn't hold her hand now, but kept a steady distance away from her. She recognized his MO: he was in full barrier-building mode.

She was caught. A polite person would back away,

respect a man's right to erect a ginormous emotional blockade between himself and the world. But as she'd acknowledged plenty of times in her career, she was in the barricade-obliteration business, and every obstacle he threw up between them emerged as an exciting challenge.

The rest of their group had migrated from the restaurant side of Latitude 33 and now stood around one of the high tables near the entrance, chatting and finishing their drinks.

"There was a waiting list to get into the restaurant, so we decided to come over here," Jane told them.

Jessie wondered if Cole would leave now. He'd looked as if he'd planned to bolt when the singing began. But he joined the others at the table, and they made room for both of them. She was glad. Even though she had to be on a case later, she wasn't ready for the evening to end. Then the sounds of a lone guitar filled the room.

"When did they start bringing in a band?" Cole asked their waitress as she removed some of the glasses and replaced a few beers.

"The owner is trying something new. The lead singer is a friend of his wife's."

Cole looked pained but resigned as he turned his gaze back to Jessie. "Do you want something besides juice?" he asked.

She shook her head. "No, I have to work tonight, and I need a clear head."

"Speaking of your work, Jessie, I bet you have some great stories," Nicole said. Jessie hadn't met her during the taping of the show, but she'd learned later Nicole usually developed the story ideas for *Just Between Us.*

"Hey, you're forgetting the rule. No work talk on Thursday nights," Eve said, her voice filled with laughter.

Nicole stood straighter. "This isn't work." Then she smiled. "But if Jessie should happen to tell some sexy story that sparks an idea for a segment, I'm not going to put my fingers in my ears and sing 'la la la.'"

"A lot of times I sign a confidentiality agreement with my clients, and most of what I do is pretty straightforward surveillance. But let's just say I have a laundry list of places I won't have sex, because of my job."

Eve glanced over at Nicole who gave her a wink. "You were right. This is what I want to hear."

"Parking lots," Jessie said promptly. "Plenty of action going on there, believe me. The park after dark, the not so deserted parts of a library. You name it, I've seen it."

"Tell us a really good one," Nicole invited.

She thought for a moment, then snapped her fingers. "Okay, I've gotten so many referrals from this man, it's hardly a secret anymore. I was hired over the phone to follow around a man's wife. He suspected she was having an affair with her 'administrative assistant.'"

"And was she?" Penny asked.

"Not that I could ever find. They didn't hit any of the usual places. No motels or out-of-town meets. Just a lot of restaurants. These people loved to eat. When I'm tailing someone I usually hang in the parking lot until they come out. So I'd watch these two arrive at some venue, stay for a while, then leave separately. I was getting zilch. Then I realized these meals they were having lasted a lot longer than a normal lunch or dinner. So I decided to take my surveillance inside."

"I can imagine where this story is headed," Nicole said.

Jessie laughed. "Oh, I don't think so."

The ladies leaned forward to hear above the synthesizer that had joined in with the guitar.

"They chose strange times to eat. This particular day, it was after the lunch rush, and I felt pretty conspicuous because there was just the couple, another man and me in the place. I try to blend into a crowd, and that's pretty tough to do when there's no one around. It got even worse after the man left. First I see the administrative assistant leave the table and head into the restroom. After a few moments, I spot my target stand. I know something's up because she also heads straight for the men's room."

Jessie had the attention of every person around the table. This must be how Eve felt, being on television and having all that interest directed solely at her.

She felt the heat of Cole's gaze. She almost wished she hadn't started this story. Maybe it wouldn't be as funny in the telling. The punch line could be a letdown. Well, she was committed now.

After taking a sip of her juice, she plunged onward. "I waited a minute or two, then decided to follow her, fully expecting to find them…enjoying one another in the public restroom."

"And did you?" Penny asked.

"No. When I walked in, she was fluffing her hair in the bathroom mirror. Looking very normal."

"Except for the fact that she was in the men's room and the previous occupant hadn't left," Cole said.

"Exactly. I looked, but there were no feet visible in the stalls. It was getting awkward. Here I was in the men's room, and I could only pretend it was an accident for so long. I really needed the goods this time, since my cover was blown. That's when my break happened. You know how those locks on the stalls don't always match up, and the door will swing open?"

"Is that what happened? Was he there?" Cole asked.

Jessie nodded.

Penny's shoulders slumped. "Well, that doesn't sound so shocking."

"Not unless you think discovering a grown man, naked and standing on top of the toilet, yet doubled over so you can't spot him above the stall door, is a little shocking."

Penny spewed her drink.

"But wait. The man started complaining that I hadn't taken his picture."

Penny's forehead wrinkled. "Now I'm confused."

"Me, too, at first. I discovered later that this was the man's wife. They'd hired me because they *wanted* to get caught doing it in a public place. I caught them the next time, as well. They like the quality of my shots so much they recommend me to a lot of their friends. Half the time when I land a new job, I don't know if I'm getting a real potential cheating client or a friend of this couple's. I just snap the picture, send it to the P.O. box and get my check."

Nicole began to laugh. "That is the weirdest story I've heard in a long time. Not sure how I can use it, but…"

"Maybe we can spin it into one of the 'keeping your relationship fresh' segments," Penny said.

Eve smiled. "Penny, I think you're going to fit in on the *Just Between Us* staff just fine."

The band finished their tune-up and the lead singer started the set off with an energetic dance number.

Nicole cleared her throat. "Ladies, there's no use expecting these men to get out on the floor for a fast dance, so I say we leave them behind and go out there and have a great time. That includes you, Jessie."

Jessie looked in Cole's direction. No help there. He leaned back in his seat as if he would appreciate the show.

With reluctant steps she followed the other ladies onto the makeshift dance floor. She felt Cole's eyes on her all the way, and she smiled to herself. And suddenly she was no longer reluctant. If he wanted a show, then a show he'd get. She liked having his eyes on her. Wanted to feel the heat of his gaze. Shifting so that she was in his line of sight, Jessie rolled her head. Her hair fell across her face, the strands sliding down her cheeks.

Dancing was pure self-expression, and lured a man, spoke to him on an elemental level. Only one other place did a woman have the same full freedom to explore her personal power: in bed. Thinking of sex gave Jessie the confidence to explore her sensuality on the dance floor. She made sure her every movement, from the gentle roll of her pelvis, to the thrust of her hips, was a promise. As she swayed, she stroked her skin.

Subtle moves. To a casual observer it would look like dancing. But to a man who'd gazed at her as Cole had when they'd played darts, with blatant hunger in his eyes, her movements were an invitation. And a warning.

With her hands she traced the neckline of her blouse and stroked slowly down her sides as she swayed to the music. A move designed to make him think of where he wanted to put his hands on her body. Touching. Caressing.

She met his gaze. The craving for her in those depths. He swallowed.

Now was the time. The payoff in the seduction dance. She projected every one of her wayward intentions through her body. Through her eyes.

And just as she saw his shoulders tense and his hands fist, as if he was about to push off from the table and join her, she took a step back. Allowed other dancers to block his view of her. Because the most important lesson she'd learned was to always leave a man wanting more.

Cole let out a breath and was finally able to drag his eyes away from the dance floor. What the hell was that? He took a swig from his beer bottle.

His stomach was in knots—so much so that he laughed to himself and shook his head. Old-fashioned, red-hot desire. That's what it was.

Now to destroy it.

It wasn't as if he'd never seen a woman dance before. But the way Jessie gyrated to the music had taken it to a whole new level. A dangerous level, because he hadn't been able to look away. Her movements were pure I-enjoy-sex carnality. Her nipples had been hard. Was she wet?

And when those slender fingers of hers had teasingly fanned down her body, the only thought in his head was how quickly he could get her off that crowded floor and into the privacy of… Hell, he didn't care where they went. Just so they were alone.

Jessie Huell was one sexy woman. It wasn't just that she had a fantastic body. It was her whole attitude. The confidence. The ease with which she talked to him. And when her gaze collided with his, he was lost. The look in her eyes…as if she were in the middle of a sexual fantasy, and he was the star… made every rational thought leave his head.

Cole wanted Jessie Huell.

It was as if everything he'd turned off, so he could concentrate on his daughters and his career, had suddenly reconnected and fired up. He was ready to make up for lost time.

For a second, he gave in to the rush. The adrenaline pumping through his system. The satisfaction knowing a hot, desirable woman wanted him.

But the woman was Jessie Huell. And this particular female came with a boatload of complications. Their past. His promise. The list could go on and on.

He'd given up complications when his ex-wife had left. It was necessary. He had two little girls depending on him to make the right decisions in his life. He owed them that and so much more.

So he'd enjoy the way the woman danced. Take the gut-level pleasure in having a woman desire him, and leave it at that.

6

JESSIE SHIFTED NERVOUSLY in her seat. Slowly, their party had dissolved into pairs. Jane with Perry, Eve with Mitchell and Nicole with Devon. And those pairs slipped into the darkness of the dance floor or shadowed corners of the bar to be alone. Penny was at the bar, chatting up a man who'd bought her a drink.

There were three specific times when interacting with the opposite sex grew really self-conscious and uncomfortable. Now was one of them. Number one on the list—when the men and women paired off, leaving a woman and the only other single male.

Jessie was alone with Cole.

The atmosphere grew taut with awareness. Cole stood beside her, big and tall and strong in a way that was uniquely male. And Cole Crawford was all man. If she put her imagination to the task, she could feel his body heat, smell that woodsy scent of his cologne. A wave of tight unease spread down her back. But she was kidding herself. It wasn't unease. It was sensual, actually. Every nerve ending was to-tally and completely aware of him.

Around them the music echoed. The beat pounding in her chest.

They both reached for their drinks at the same time. Their knuckles brushed. Lingered a little longer than necessary. She took a sip, needing the chill of the juice to cool her. This whole waiting for him to do something felt so familiar, as if she'd done this exact same thing before.

In fact, she had. But she wasn't that girl who watched as life passed her by. She set her glass down and turned to face Cole.

Did any man look better than he did at this moment? The flashing blue and red dance lights glinted along his firm jaw, highlighting the sexy fullness of his bottom lip. The dimness of the bar masked the expression in his eyes, but his body let her know he'd stayed beside her for something other than the music.

She met his gaze head-on, allowing her eyes to drift to his mouth the way his gaze had drifted to her lips earlier. The message she sent him couldn't be more clear. But just in case…

"I don't make the first move," she told him, her stare direct.

His shoulders stiffened. His knuckles turned white as he gripped the beer bottle tighter.

Of course, she'd said she didn't make the first move, but that was meant to be one.

Which led to awkward situation number two: that

moment right before a kiss. Or a potential kiss. Or the offer of a kiss that was turned down flat.

Her heartbeat quickened, and she heard the sound of her blood rushing in her ears.

These moments were a kind of torture.

"I do." Cole shoved his beer bottle onto the table, then shifted toward her. He raised his hands to cup her face, his thumb caressing her chin. Her lower lip. His eyes narrowed, focused solely on her. Almost as if he were searching.

This was it. Cole Crawford, the boy of her dreams, the man of her private fantasies, was finally going to kiss her. She held her breath in anticipation. She no longer cared if reality destroyed fantasy.

He lowered his head. Slowly. Torturously slow. Her eyes drifted shut with the first brush of his mouth. His lips were soft and gentle against hers. But she didn't want soft and gentle. She licked the seam of his lips, and with a groan, his kiss deepened. He sank his fingers into her hair. His tongue plunged into her mouth. He tasted good, like danger and pure heat.

This was way better than anything her imagination could have conjured. Cole's hands lowered and he dragged her to his chest. She wrapped her arms around his neck, the tips of her fingers brushing the hair at his nape, drawing him closer still. His kiss grew hungry, his fingers restless, and Jessie felt how much Cole wanted her.

"The things I'd like to do to you," she whispered. The things she'd like him to do to her.

Her breathing grew ragged. *This*. This was what she needed. It had been so long since she'd felt the ecstasy of having a man sexually attracted to her. The beating her pride had taken after finding her fiancé in bed with another woman was forgotten.

"We have to get out of here," Cole growled, and she felt the rumble of his chest against hers. The desire in his voice made her body grow urgent and hypersensitive.

A woman's laugh from the table beside them broke them apart. Jessie tried to scramble out of Cole's arms, but he held her close.

"Should we tell the others?"

He shook his head. "They'll figure it out."

"I have to be at work in thirty minutes," she told him, not bothering to hide her disappointment. They didn't have a lot of time.

He released her. His expression darkened. The heat surrounding them waned. "I'll walk you to your car," he said, his voice tight. Strained. She thought she may have heard him say, "Just as well," under his breath.

"That's not necessary."

He lifted an eyebrow. "It's nighttime. I walk a woman to her car."

Jessie smiled to herself, relishing having Cole get all protective. Protective of her. She should tell him she had extensive training in aikido and that the gun she'd mentioned while playing darts was actually in her purse. But she wasn't stupid. A woman alone was a much easier target than one with a man. More to the point, she wasn't stupid enough to turn down time with Cole.

He took her hand, his fingers twining with hers. He felt solid and warm as he led her quickly through the restaurant.

The cool night air hit her heated skin, giving her goose bumps. She'd blame the fact that her nipples were now beaded under the lavender blouse on the weather, too. Neither she nor Cole said a word as they retraced their steps to the TV station.

He led her to the parking lot, where they officially reached awkward scenario number three. They'd been left alone. They'd kissed. Now would they leave it at that?

"There's still a lot of cars here," she said, glancing around and trying to make conversation.

"Staff has to stay on twenty-four–seven to keep the station running. You never know when something might happen."

"That's my car over there. The black one," she told him, pointing to a vehicle bathed in the amber overhead light. Could this conversation become any more stilted? If one of them even mentioned the weather she'd bolt.

They stopped at her car door, neither saying a

thing, the atmosphere intense. "Okay, then…" She began to rummage through her purse for her keys. "It was good seeing you again, Cole."

She glanced up, meeting his eyes.

And almost dropped her keys, her purse and her composure.

A look of utter wanting haunted his eyes. Jessie forgot about first moves and awkwardness. She wrapped her arms around him. With a groan he hauled her up against him. Their lips met.

Jessie longed to drag her hands over every part of his body. She loved the feel of his muscular arms, his tight butt. She hooked her leg around his calf, and felt the strain of his muscles. Here was a man about to lose control. She almost smiled, reveling in the sensual power she had. Relishing his need for her.

Cole kissed her eyes, her cheeks, her chin. When his lips, then his tongue, found the skin above her collarbone, she gasped, arching upward. Her hips jutted into his. The hard ridge of his erection pressed against her most sensitive spot. Jessie moaned, not caring how it sounded.

And he grew harder. "Jessie, what you do to me." His voice was a ragged whisper.

His fingers wrapped around her leg, gently drawing it up around his waist. Cole caressed the skin above her knee, his hand questing higher.

She shivered, twining her fingers in his hair and drawing his earlobe into her mouth.

"I want to touch all of you," he said insistently.

He turned her so that she faced her Impala. Bracing her arms on the roof of the car, she let out a low moan as his lips found the erogenous place below her ear. With one hand caressing her breast, the other slowly moving down her waist, Cole made Jessie feel decadent.

When his hand found her hip, he pulled her to him. She again gasped, this time at the amazing sensation of Cole's cock pressed firmly against her bottom. "That's better," he whispered.

He slid his hand down her shirt…seeking. Frustration filled her. She was impatient with straps, hooks, underwires and elastic. "I hate my bras."

His breath fluttered against her neck when he chuckled. "No, it's sexy." Finally, *finally* Cole's hand cupped her breast. Her nipple hardened even further, and she rolled her head back to rest on Cole's shoulder. Her eyes drifted shut in pleasure.

Jessie began to pant. "Cole," she pleaded. Not sure what she intended to say.

His other hand slid up her thigh, not stopping at the barrier of her panties, but slipping inside. Her legs began to quiver.

"You're so wet," he said as he stroked her. His finger found her clit, circled around it. She cried out, backing harder against his penis.

"Damn, Jessie. You turn me the hell on."

She opened her eyes, seeing her face reflected in

the car window. Her hair was a mess, tumbled about her face. Her lips were slightly parted, and swollen from their kiss. She looked a little wild. Like a woman enjoying her man.

She smiled at her reflection. And *how* did she plan to enjoy that man. Jessie almost laughed. She was actually with Cole Crawford. Mr. Perfect. And he was doing *everything* perfectly.

He stroked her. A long caress touching and teasing every inch of her. She bucked against him.

Cole groaned. "Do that again."

"Then *you* do that again," she told him, her voice filled with satisfaction. Satisfaction knowing she could make him as hot and bothered as he made her.

He licked the back of her neck as he plunged his whole hand into her panties. He cupped her. She gasped. His thumb gently caressed her clit as his finger pierced her wet core. Mimicking sex. Teasing her. Making her want more. And she did want more. She wanted it all.

His other hand continued to stroke and mold her breast. Her nipple ached to feel the touch of his fingers. The warmth of his mouth.

He added another finger to her slick core. Her muscles surged around him. "Oh, Cole…"

"What?" he asked, his mouth traveling to her earlobe, giving it a tug with his teeth. "Tell me. I want to hear your voice."

"If you don't stop, I'm going to…"

"Go. Come, Jessie. I've wanted to watch you come since I saw you dance tonight."

She opened her eyes, meeting his gaze in the reflection of her window. His jaw was set, his expression determined. He added another finger.

"Ahhh," she groaned. Her eyes closed as the force of her orgasm hit her. She ground against him as wave after wave of pleasure raced through her body.

Afterward, she sagged against the car. Her legs felt shaky, but there was still a hard penis poking her from behind. And right now, all she could think about was getting her hands wrapped around him. Energy began to chase away her orgasm-induced lethargy.

Jessie reached to stroke him.

He blocked her hand. "But—"

"You have to get to work," he reminded her.

"I can be late," she said, her voice coming out husky and tired. Like a woman well satisfied.

The muscles of his arms tightened. Then he turned her to face him and lightly kissed her lips. Although the kiss thrilled her, she knew what it was by the way he didn't linger. How the hunger had vanished. A goodbye kiss.

"I want to make you feel good," she told him, sucking his lower lip into her mouth.

"I can't have you lose a job because of me." Where was the bad boy who'd skip an assembly with a wink? "When I make love to you I want to go slow so we can do it all night."

Ah, there he was. Now, what kind of woman would argue with that?

He looked behind his shoulder briefly, then his dark eyes met hers once more. "And I don't want any chance of an interruption."

With reluctance, Jessie bent down to retrieve her keys and purse. When had she dropped those? Probably sometime between Cole thrusting his hand under her shirt or his fingers down her panties.

Jessie adjusted her clothes quickly. She couldn't help the small smile that played around her lips. This was definitely not what she'd expected when she'd been awakened this morning by the ringing of the telephone.

She slid into the front seat of her car, and Cole shut the door behind her. He nodded when he heard her lock the door. He stayed in the lot until she'd pulled into the late-night traffic.

Her skin tingled. Her body felt warm all over. A moment ago, she'd been worn-out and lethargic. Now her energy was boundless. She'd just experienced one of the most explosive orgasms, with all her clothes on. Or with all her clothes off. She couldn't wait to get Cole naked and in bed with her.

When I make love with you...

The promise behind his words made her hands tremble on the steering wheel.

That was a promise, wasn't it? His words also sounded distinctly like a line. A line to get her out of there. Jessie's shoulders tensed and her fingers tapped on the stick shift as she waited for the light to change. Maybe she should take a hint from her on-the-job techniques, and put herself in Cole's situation. They'd been out in the open. In his place of business. They'd risked enough. She sighed and eased back against her seat. Okay, that hadn't been a brush-off.

Then it hit her. She'd pretty much had sex in the exact place she'd always said she would avoid. A parking lot. With a rueful laugh, she shifted her car into third and headed to her job.

COLE STOOD IN THE PARKING LOT, dragging in deep gulps of air. He stayed until he couldn't spot the red of Jessie's taillights anymore. He stayed until he could breathe normally again. Those little gasps and moans had nearly been his undoing.

He'd almost hiked up that sexy, short black skirt of hers, pushed her panties down, raised her hips and entered her from behind.

What the hell was he doing?

He covered his face with his hands. Hadn't he just reminded himself that he had two little girls who counted on him not to make idiotic choices?

Making it with Jessie in the parking lot was not the best choice.

He stalked to his car, feeling frustrated with himself, frustrated in general. His need for her still ached.

Jessie Huell surprised him. Without a doubt, she was the sexiest woman he'd ever seen. He unlocked his car and jammed his key into the ignition. Instantly, another thought struck him. About what he'd almost done to her before the— Dammit.

Dammit, he was acting reckless.

He hated the recklessness within him. He'd battled it on a daily basis his entire life. His father had said Cole was born bad. And he'd almost started to believe it himself, until Jessie.

He'd always suspected there was fire between them. And he'd stayed away after…after that night. He scrubbed his hand down his face. After she'd saved his life, he'd made a promise to her father. That he would never involve Jessie in anything of his again. He'd kept that promise, despite seeing the hurt in her eyes when he returned for his senior year in high school and basically had nothing to do with her.

But they were adults now. He wasn't that hell-bent teenager anymore. Promises could have expiration dates. He almost laughed at that twisted logic.

But where could it go? He had nothing to offer Jessie. He *knew* her, despite what she'd said on the show. She'd want a relationship, a man who could offer her more than a few quick rolls between the sheets. She'd want lazy Saturday mornings. Talks of dreams that went long into the night. She deserved it. All of it. A secret pang of longing hit him just then. One time he'd wanted those things, too.

What would she get with him? Nothing but stolen moments in a parking lot.

With harsh control he battled his wicked, restless need for her and put all thoughts of Jessie aside.

7

FRIDAY MORNING CAME EARLY for Cole after a sleepless night thinking of Jessie, naked and in the backseat of his car. And he'd never wanted to have sex in that cramped space before.

He finally threw back the sheets and packed. He'd be leaving for his sister's place in Dunner, Georgia, right after the show closed. It was funny that his sister, who'd always clamored to move to the big city, had actually settled in a place smaller than Thrasher after her marriage. But then love had a habit of making someone change their mind. About a lot of things.

He was taking the girls camping, and all three had been looking forward to it. Even though his cabin was only forty-five minutes away from Dunner, they hadn't made it there since the girls had started soccer. But now with the season ending, there was nothing to stop him from romping through the tall Georgia pines, roasting marshmallows under the stars and catching up with his girls.

Leaving Susan and Schyler, his seven-year-old twin daughters, with his sister and heading back to

Atlanta every Monday morning was a bleak reminder of who and what depended on him. The situation wasn't ideal, but the girls were happy with his
sister and her family. With his crazy schedule, ar-
ranging day care for his twins had been impossible.

If only the lottery money would come in. He
could quit his job and raise the girls full-time.

Cole stopped himself. He wasn't a man for speculation or fantasy. Either would be reckless. He didn't
have the money yet, and Liza turning down their
offer to settle for a smaller sum meant a trial was
pretty much imminent. Lawyers' fees and court costs
would eat at even more of the winnings.

So basically, his choices were thinking about getting sued or about not getting screwed. No wonder
he couldn't sleep.

First up, the not getting sued part. Cole, Eve,
Nicole, Jane and Zach had an early morning meeting
with their lawyer, Jenna Hamilton. Too bad after the
show hadn't fit with their lawyer's schedule.

He pulled into the full parking lot. The early
morning news staff hadn't left yet, so he was forced
to torture himself and park where Jessie's Impala had
sat the night before. The memory of a woman's
heated sigh flashed across his senses. And despite
being five seconds away from turning off the ignition, he turned up the music.

He'd spent all night being only a breath away
from semihard to total performance mode. No way

could he spend the day that way. That was when the temptation to give in to his recklessness was its most fierce.

His body tormented him. His mind explored last night's possibilities. Outside of the car. In the car. Across the hood. None of those ideas seemed bad right now.

Cole took a deep breath, then made himself think of being called into the station manager's office to explain a lengthy incident report filed by security. He'd been damn lucky no one had caught them. The guard swept the perimeter of the building and parking lot at least once every two hours.

Cole shook his head, grabbed his briefcase and headed toward the conference room. Jane, Nicole and the cameraman, Zach, were already sitting around the large oak table.

Jane and Nicole exchanged glances and laughed.

"Glad you could finally make it, Cole. Late night?" Jane asked.

This he would not be a part of. He shrugged and did his best to appear neutral. "Not particularly," he replied, sounding noncommittal and a little confused by the question.

He saw Jane frown slightly in disappointment. Good. He should have used this precise tactic after that embarrassing article surfaced. Then maybe he wouldn't have had to be teased for the last few weeks.

Eve breezed into the room, followed by Jenna Hamilton.

The lawyer walked to the head of the table, but did not sit down. "I just received word that Ms. Skinner has rejected our offer to settle for the small portion of the winnings. It looks as if we'll have to go to trial."

Nicole slumped in her chair. "I was really hoping it wouldn't come to this."

This was why he hadn't allowed himself to speculate on those winnings. Cole could see no point in it. But the truth of the matter was he had to swallow his own disappointment. Even though he didn't think Liza truly deserved the money, he was more than willing to offer up a settlement to get his own share sooner.

"What's next?" he asked.

"Well, you need to decide whether or not you want to file a counterclaim."

"On what grounds?" Eve asked.

Jenna's expression grew somber. She clearly had a love for the subject. "Libel, for one. We may have a case that your professional reputations have been tarnished somewhat. There's also lost interest on the money had you all been able to receive your winnings earlier. Filing our own claim would delay a trial, which would be to your advantage. Her funds have got to be running low."

"She didn't have a lot of savings. I wonder how long she can hold out," Jane said.

Jane, Eve and Liza had been best friends since the sixth grade. Cole knew, because that's all they'd talked about some days. God, he could still recall the way their conversations went when the show was just up and running.

"Do you remember Greg Grimler asking you to dance?"

"I Googled nerdy Tommy Hardon—remember him from Mrs. Nease's trig class? Oh, my God, he's hot now!"

Cole winced, once again feeling a testosterone vacuum. Even the memories of those conversations were painful. The silver lining: he could take some comfort in the fact that Jane could predict Liza's behavior pretty well. If she thought Liza would cave soon, Liza would probably cave soon.

Jenna shifted her paperwork on the conference table. "Ordinarily, it would be to your advantage to drag our feet during the discovery phase, hoping Liza's money would run out and she'd take the settlement. But with the eight-month deadline the Lottery Commission has you under fast approaching, you're facing your own sword of Damocles."

He didn't know what the sword of dama— whatever it was, but it sounded painful. He must have slept through that class after an all-nighter at the garage. But others around the table groaned, so it had to be bad.

"However, it's my professional opinion that a

counterclaim may do you more harm. We're on solid ground with the case itself. The fact that you offered Ms. Skinner a settlement shows good faith on your part. Filing your own claim could look petty or vindictive to a jury."

Cole glanced around the room, seeking consensus. Everyone shook their head.

Eve took it from there. "I don't think that will be necessary."

Jenna nodded and pulled a set of papers from her briefcase. "Okay, next step—interrogatories. These are just a series of questions that I'll turn over to Kev— Uh, Ms. Skinner's lawyer. Don't worry about format, just answer as best you can. I'll have a clerk type these up."

The meeting droned on and on. Cole tried to put this situation in perspective. He should be feeling great instead of sitting here miserable. He'd literally won the lottery. The money was being held up, but eventually he'd receive some of his winnings. Liza wouldn't be so petty as to drag it out so long no one got anything. Based on his own track record, Cole hadn't always been a good judge of character, but he'd admired her at one time.

He should also be feeling damn lucky about Jessie. He'd reconnected with a woman who clearly wanted him.

Eight hours later, he was speeding along the Georgia highway, surrounded by a tall canopy of trees draped with Spanish moss. He lost himself in the beauty of the wildflowers, the untamed flow of the rivers. The great out-of-doors was the one place where he truly knew himself. And felt comfortable with his flaws, but also discovered his strengths. He'd left his small hometown to make something of himself. He traveled to Dunner each Friday night to be with the best part of him that he'd left behind. His daughters.

JESSIE WAS NOT THE TYPE of person who'd wait around for a man to call. She'd done enough of that with her fiancé. So what if she'd had no word from Cole since Thursday? The women from his office had told her he left Friday after the show to visit with his daughters. No reason to stress. Or feel uncomfortable.

And the fact that it was now Monday. Afternoon… Still nothing to worry about. Cole was just being considerate. He knew she worked late nights and slept in.

Okay, damn. She'd thought about why Cole hadn't called. But she wouldn't do it again. She had a case to work. A very boring case. Background checks and DMV look-throughs.

The phone rang, and Jessie smiled when she saw that the ID displayed the call letters of the TV station. She answered the phone with what she hoped was a sultry yet utterly normal hello.

"Hi, it's Nicole from the station. Jessie, I've thought about you all weekend."

Her shoulders dropped. At least someone had been thinking of her.

"I have an idea. I think you'd be great for a special segment all your own."

"Oh, I don't—"

"Before you say no, hear me out. That keeping your marriage fresh idea was just the beginning. I guarantee you that no one has your particular angle. Who knew people hired a P.I. to take their picture playing around in a public place with their actual spouse? I bet I could get three great segments on your fling ideas alone. We've gotten excellent viewer comments, and the forums on the Web site are hopping with the topic. That's just the stuff I've brainstormed and jotted down. Together we could come up with even more."

"I'm still not—"

"Let's talk. Why don't I drop by your office?" It wasn't really a question.

Clearly, Nicole wasn't going to take no for an answer. As annoying as it was, Jessie liked that about her.

"I'm doing background research today at home. I live in Grant Park."

"No problem. An hour and a half work for you? The show will be over."

After giving Nicole her address, Jessie rolled out of bed and plodded toward the bathroom. She'd have time to catch a shower and straighten up before Nicole arrived.

She maintained a small storefront office for meeting clients, but the bulk of her work she did from home. After her shower, Jessie donned her usual black. This time long pants and a short-sleeved knit top. She brushed her hair into a ponytail, and took the stairs two at a time to the spare bedroom she used as an in-home office. Since she didn't know how much of her time would be taken with Nicole, she headed straight to her desk, a beautiful wood secretary she'd found in an estate sale. She kept her computer inside, and after powering up, she put her search engine to work. Thoughts of Cole kept slipping into her mind. Should she Google him?

Jessie jumped when the doorbell rang. She could get so lost in her research. No telling how many times her guest had rung the doorbell, so Jessie quickly made her way to the door. Nicole greeted her with a smile, so it couldn't have been too long of a wait. "I'm so glad you're going to do this. I know the buzz on this will be fantastic."

"Iced tea?" Jessie offered as they strolled into her study.

"No thanks," Nicole said as she looked around. "I love these houses in Grant Park."

"I was lucky to find it. It has that smaller town feel that reminded me of home, but easy access to downtown Atlanta. The previous owners lived here a long time, but hadn't updated it. Powder blue shag carpeting covered the floor."

Nicole looked at the hardwood floor Jessie kept to a shine. "That's a crime. These hardwood floors are beautiful."

"Thanks, I did it myself."

Her expression changed, grew impressed. "How did you get everything done while trying to start up your own business?"

"Humiliation and anger did a number on my sleeping habits."

Nicole raised an eyebrow.

"I caught my fiancé in bed with another woman. She was a dispatcher at the police station where we all worked. Obviously, the man liked dipping his pen in the company ink. I quit the man and my job on the force all on the same day. But I decided, just because I hadn't found my dream man, it didn't mean I'd give up on my dream house."

Keith, the cheating bastard, had suggested they sell it and split the proceeds. No way. The threat of damage to his penis had him backing off.

"During the day I refurbished the house. Stripping and staining the hardwood floors. Painting the walls and returning the beauty to this home. At night I worked my cases."

"How did you become a private detective?"

Her breath came out as a sigh. "That man dropped so many tells, and if I'd just looked under the surface…" Jessie swallowed, urged her heartbeat to return to normal. No woman should ever come home to find her man's ass pumping forward and a woman writhing in *her* bed. Hopefully, with her new line of work, Jessie would prevent other women from seeing that sight. Not the pain of reality, but there were some images a woman could never erase from her mind.

Jessie glanced toward Nicole. "Anyway, I almost made the biggest mistake of my life. My police training gave me the skill set to help other women not be as big of an idiot as I was. It's easy to ignore all the little hints. I was in love. I wanted it to work. Blah, blah, blah. But when you get the goods from a professional…"

"It's easier to believe." Nicole filled in for her.

"Exactly. I quit my job on the force the same day I told my new ex-fiancé I was keeping the house and he could forget his share of the down payment." Keith, the cheating bastard, owed her. "He wisely kept his mouth shut. After sitting for the private-detective exam, I used the money from hocking my engagement ring to pay for my P.I. license."

Nicole sat back against the cushion of the couch. "There's a segment right there. Claiming your Own Life While Leaving the Louse Behind. I'm so glad this is working out. Cole is bound to like these ideas. He was such a bear today. And he's never like that. Of course, you would know. You grew up together."

For some reason, the idea of Cole being a bear made her smile. Could she have been the one to bring out those grizzly qualities in the man? Had he been experiencing the same kind of sleepless nights and ragged sexual frustration? She liked the thought of that. She really did.

Nicole leaned forward. "You wouldn't want to share any juicy tidbit about Cole."

"I don't know." Jessie stood, trying to distance herself from this situation.

"Come on, the guy's like a rock. That article saying he had his finger on the pulse of Atlanta's women was the first time any of us have ever been able to get under his skin. He takes teasing so poorly, I can't help wanting to do it more."

"Unfortunately, he's always been calm and cool." On one hand, Jessie felt she should stick with her hometown boy. Then she remembered he hadn't called. "But there is this one thing. He was really embarrassed about it."

"Tell me," Nicole urged.

"This is hardly anything, but when he was sixteen he failed his driver's test. He messed up parallel parking."

Nicole laughed and clapped her hands. "I can use that."

COLE HADN'T BEEN ABLE TO concentrate at all on Monday. Erotic dreams could do that to a man. Tuesday started out only marginally better. At least Nicole had brought some good ideas to the production meeting, but at the expense of his sanity, because Jessie Huell had been featured prominently in the discussion. It was as if everything around him had conspired to dig that woman out of his subconscious, where she belonged.

The meeting was over and they'd reverted to chitchat. He stood to leave, but Eve placed a hand on his arm.

"Cole, we've been getting some interesting e-mails about the way the chairs and couches are placed on the set. Apparently it's distracting, and viewers would prefer it if they were, oh, what's that word I'm looking for? You know, where the everything is set up the same distance apart in two lines…."

"Parallel?" he offered.

"That's it. Thanks." A wicked glint entered her eyes. "I'm surprised you knew that word."

Eve passed by him to leave the conference room. Since when did she have time to worry about the set? Women were flat-out weird.

After lunch, and more thoughts of Jessie, dammit, Nicole popped her head into his office. "I was hoping you could do me a favor. Devon took his car into the shop, so he dropped me off and borrowed mine. That printer downtown completed one of our promo jobs. Could you take me over there?"

"Sure," he said, glancing down at his appointment book. "You want to go now?"

Nicole bit her lip as if she was worried. "You know what, you'd have to parallel park outside the front. Never mind. I'll ask someone else." She turned to go.

Cole surged to his feet. Impossible. "Wait."

Her lips were twisting, as if she was trying not to smile. What was going on here? Then he remembered. Nicole had spent time interviewing Jessie. She'd sold him out.

"Jessie told you," he stated incredulously.

"Just how many times did you fail your test?" Nicole held up first two, then three fingers.

"Once." He had a hard time not saying that through clenched teeth.

"If it makes you feel any better, that was the worst thing she could come up with."

He doubted that.

Nicole's smile faded. "Shame you caught on so quickly, because Penny had some great stuff lined up."

"I was beginning to think I was in an episode of *The Office*."

Nicole turned to leave.

"Oh, and remind everyone I'll be doing the driving to the station's mandatory fun day," he told her. He heard her laughter all the way down the hall.

Cole was in the mood for a little payback. He looked at the clock. Jessie would probably still be asleep. Perfect. He dialed the number.

8

COLE CRAWFORD SAT silently beside her in the car.

Did he plan to talk?

Jessie flicked her gaze toward him for about the thousandth time, just to make sure he wasn't asleep. As was often the case when she was on a job, it was after midnight. Still nothing. But his eyes were open. He merely sat there. Stoically.

She didn't really know what to do. He'd called. Woken her up, in fact.

Cole had caught on to her slipping some inside information to the ladies he worked with. His tone was stern, but she could tell he wasn't actually angry about it. In fact, hearing his voice had reminded her how much she wanted to see him again. To see if what they'd experienced together in the parking lot was a one-time thing, brought on by memories and long suppressed emotions, or true desire.

She'd invited him along on her stakeout tonight, and he'd accepted. And now this. Silence.

The Speculation Game tempted, but lately all she wanted to speculate about was Cole. And that could be very dangerous. She had firsthand knowledge of his skills below the belt, and it wouldn't take much to drift into the land of Fabricatia.

"You know, we can talk. We're not at the point where we have to be quiet," Jessie told him as she headed the car to one of Atlanta's suburban greenbelts.

The light turned yellow, and Jessie slowed to a stop. She placed the car in Park, then shifted in her seat to face him. The streetlights cast a shaft of light across his face. She met his eyes.

And swallowed.

A look of such hunger, such passion burned in his gaze.

Oh.

Jessie swiftly turned, fumbling to get the car back into Drive. Beads of sweat broke out across her forehead, ran down her back. Her nipples hardened, and she nibbled on her lip. That was why he was so quiet. Cole wanted her. Bad. Stoically bad.

Despite her pounding heart, and her blood turning warm and sluggish in her veins, she felt light. Gratified. Jessie also felt excited and powerful, knowing Cole wanted her to the level his eyes promised. Frankly, he didn't have to talk ever again. Just look at her with that dark carnal need and she'd be good forever.

A thrill of anticipation soared through her, from her head to her toes. She'd be enjoying Cole tonight. Although that preview after the sports bar had been great, she was ready for the feature film. With popcorn. Suddenly, she couldn't wait for this job to be over.

She pulled into a parking space of an all-night grocery store, and reached for her camera bag. "This is it."

"I thought you said they were meeting in the park?" he asked, his voice husky with arousal.

"They are, but the park closes after dark. They see my car there, they'll know they won't be alone. We hike it. C'mon, it's not far."

Cole opened his door and stepped out. He walked around to her side. Jessie spotted the bulge in his jeans, and her thoughts zipped to the other night in the parking lot. She'd felt his erection against her. A wave of desire flooded her now. She wanted to feel that way again.

He took the not-so-heavy camera bag from her shoulder and looped it over his own. His fingertips grazing the bare skin of her arm.

She could carry her own bag. Cole knew it. Cole knew she knew it. He just chose to carry it for her. That thrill slid through her once more.

The autumn air felt cool against her skin. The smell of pine and oak lingered in the slight breeze. Above them, the stars were washed out by the city lights. They headed for the park, their footsteps almost silent along the pavement.

The bright lights of the grocery store faded, leaving the night broken up by streetlamps. With its large trees, the park would be even darker. Lots of places to hide. Jessie and Cole passed through the flowered entrance and into the deserted playground area.

"It will take a good fifteen minutes before we really get our night eyes." Okay, why was she telling him this? Cole was a survivalist. That was something Nicole had mentioned in passing. The man could probably navigate the outdoors quicker and easier than a coffee addict could find a Starbucks.

Jessie stopped and turned toward him. Why not put those skills of his to good use? "In a minute we can scope for a place to hide. Think trees. Somewhere we don't have to crouch. Big enough for both of us. I don't expect the couple to get here for at least an hour."

He nodded. Looking around.

Jessie loved the evening air. As a cop, she'd always enjoyed the night beat. The city was different after sunset. The energy changed. Most people didn't know the nocturnal Atlanta.

She walked toward the push-type merry-go-round and sat down on it, waiting for her eyes to adjust. Crickets and their songs were usually her only company, but tonight she had Cole. She felt warmed by the knowledge, and willed the hour to fly by so she could be even more alone with him.

The round metal platform of the toy rotated as Cole sat down beside her. So close she felt the heat of his body, yet so far she couldn't pass off an accidental touch. He stretched out his long legs. A leaf crunched under his shoe and he brought the merry-go-round to a stop. The energy shifted. A charged flow zipped between them. Nothing but a safety bar and the Atlanta evening air separated them. She faced him, wanting to read the expression in his eyes, knowing it was too dark.

"I don't need my eyes to see you in the dark." His hand came up to cup her cheek.

She swallowed. Although Jessie said she didn't make the first move, she'd given him that wide-open invitation. Although she'd relived that kiss in the bar, that mind-blowing orgasm he'd given her in the parking lot, she would wait. Even though he'd become something like an addiction, and she was dying for another taste, Jessie would not move.

If he wanted her he'd have to come and get her.

"You make the sexiest sounds when you come. They turn me on. I want to hear them again."

She wanted to make them again.

"We shouldn't do this."

"Probably not."

"Do you mind?"

"Hell no."

Then his lips were on hers, his hands on her shoulders. He urged her lips open, and she squirmed as his smooth tongue filled her mouth. This was no gentle, exploring kiss. This was all heat. Cole's tongue twined with hers. He tightened his grasp, pulling her shoulders and pulling her close. She moaned. Yes.

His hands, his mouth, his whole body were making good on the promise that had been in his eyes earlier.

Cole pressed against her, and she rolled back against the cool metal of the merry-go-round. Ducking under the safety bar, he followed her down, his body settling beside hers. Cole's mouth lowered, gliding down the slope of her neck. His tongue caressing her sensitive skin.

"You thought about me this weekend." His voice was tight with strain.

She nodded, not wanting to waste her energy on something stupid like talking.

"Good." His whisper was low and rough and did all kinds of tantalizing things to her senses.

He tugged her black T-shirt free from her pants, then slipped his hand inside. Jessie sucked in a breath as Cole's questing fingers slid along her stomach. Moving higher. Skimming her ribs. She groaned and dragged his mouth back to her when he cupped her breast.

Her breasts were heavy, aching to feel his touch. He slipped below the wire of her bra. "Tell me this is black," he said, his breath warm against her cheek. Her body tingled in response.

"It is."

"I'll have to look for myself, to see if you're telling me the truth."

"I'm counting on that."

With a low, utterly male groan, he pushed the cup

over her breast. Smoothed her shirt out of his way. Her nipple tightened from the chill of the air. Then Cole lowered his head and licked a lazy path around the tip. Her body jolted, lifting toward him. Their movements caused the merry-go-round to make a slow spin on its axis.

Then he stopped.

She opened her eyes and saw his crooked smile. Her eyes had fully adjusted to the darkness, and were ready to do nothing but soak him in…imprint the set of his strong jaw, the rugged softness of his lips into her memory.

"Tell me, Jessie, where do people usually… meet?"

It took her a moment to clear her head. Her skin practically sizzled from the rush his question gave her. "The swings."

"Really?"

Jessie heard the doubt in his voice and grinned. She knew why he asked. "Don't worry. After the first time I saw what people attempted on that swing set, I checked it out on the Internet. Those seats are reinforced with steel. Can take up to three thousand pounds."

He raised from her, braced himself from off the merry-go-round and gazed down at her. "What about impact?"

She laughed, loving where his thoughts headed. Naughty boys grew up to be naughty men. "I think it can handle us and whatever…force we might give it."

"Come," he said, the word a carnal invitation.

Jessie felt naughty. Uninhibited. Playing where they weren't supposed to. She almost had the urge to yell, "Race you!"

Instead she collected her camera bag and placed her hand in Cole's. His warm fingers engulfed hers, tugged her upward. She stood beside him, her lips at his chin. Inside, she quaked with sexual need. He was about to draw her to the swing set, lay her across the seat and make love to her.

Would that be considered making love? Those words evoked a bed, silken sheets. Maybe a candle.

What she was about to do with Cole was not that polite. It would be erotic, adventurous sex.

He grasped her chin, tugged her lips toward his and kissed her. The air rushed from her body as he pulled her against him. Jessie loved the hardness of his chest. His thighs. She lifted her leg and hooked it around his waist, feeling the stiffness of his erection. She couldn't wait to feel it, feel him, inside her.

He scooped her up into his arms and stalked toward the swings. He set her down in a seat. She wound her arms around the chains and moved her thighs apart to accommodate him. Cole stepped between her legs and pressed into her. The bulge of his penis rubbed against her clit. She gasped at the delicious friction.

He took a slow step back, then forward, mimicking the movements of a swing. Duplicating the thrusts of sex.

She wanted more. She hated her clothes, her bra and her panties. She wanted to be naked. In his arms. Jessie slid her legs around his hips, making it more difficult for him to move.

"I want you," she said, her voice raspy but strong. She knew what she wanted. He was right in front of her.

"I've been waiting to hear you say that."

His fingers settled at the button of her jeans and she shivered. The unmistakable sound of her zipper moving down joined the other sounds of the night. The high-pitched call of a bird. The squeak of the swing. The harshness of their breathing.

A beam of light streaked through the trees. Headlights. They broke apart instantly, except for his hand. Cole reached for hers and never let go. He made for the bushes, crouching as he went. Jessie followed him. With a quick tug, he pulled her toward him and they concealed themselves behind the greenery. Their breath coming out in pants.

"Yes," she urged. "This is the exact place I've used for cover."

Cole dropped her hand, and a coldness seeped into her fingers, which had been warm from his touch. Jessie shook off the feeling and quickly fastened her jeans. Dammit.

"So, you've been to this park before?" he asked, a teasing note lacing his words. "How come you had us come so early to scope out the place?"

Caught. "Maybe what I wanted was to scope you out." She might as well shoot for honesty.

His palms found her hips, and Cole caressed the skin above her waistband.

She pulled her combo camera binoculars out of the bag. The equipment had cost her, but it was worth not having the hassle of carrying two devices around her neck. She trained the lens on the ironwork entrance. "Now, stop, you're distracting me," she told him with a laugh. Inviting Cole to join her had been one of those spur of the moment decisions she was not known for. He was definitely proving to be hell on her detecting work.

A large black bundle of energy rumbled across the park. The dog barked as he rolled in the grass, getting leaves stuck in his coat.

"There boy, there." A man's voice, deep and low, soothed the animal.

"It's just a guy walking his dog," Cole whispered beside her.

Jessie shook her head. Something wasn't right. She felt it in her gut. And she was a firm believer in her gut. "Who drives their dog to a closed park to walk it? Why not just walk in the neighborhood? No, he's using the dog for cover."

Although the man and his dog weren't the clients

she was being paid to snap pictures of, she switched to camera mode and took a few shots anyway.

Dog and man walked on, looking innocent. At least the dog did. Something about the man still seemed suspicious to her.

"Should we stay here?"

"Even with the added company, I don't want to risk missing the couple we came for. According to the husband, they only meet once a week." On her book-club night. Although, the man didn't appear too shaken up about his wife's possible infidelity. He seemed more interested in Jessie's cameras and shot techniques.

Nighttime photos were tricky. They often came out unfocused, blurry, or even worse, lacking the kind of convincing detail needed in her profession. She'd armed herself with the best equipment, but on a near moonless night like tonight, she needed a long exposure time to soak up as much ambient light as possible. That meant a steady hand and patience.

During Jessie's initial meeting with the husband, he'd asked about the quality of her prints. As if maybe he'd tried to capture a few night photos himself and failed.

Jessie let out a sigh. She'd missed all the clues and they were practically shouting at her, "Hello, this isn't what it seems."

"What is it?" Cole asked.

"I just realized these people are probably a couple of Talbarts." Jessie could kick herself for not being on her game. She'd blame it on the fact that she'd been awed by all the TV stuff. Or Cole's kiss. Or the way his fingers drove her to an I-can't-wait-to-see-what-else-he-has-in-store-for-me orgasm.

Oh, yeah, she'd be happy to lay blame for her lackluster efforts with this client, elsewhere—that is, if she wasn't in the business of assigning blame squarely where it belonged.

Jessie wasn't an excuse maker. That was one of the tenets she began with when she'd started her P.I. firm. Her advice would be short and sweet, since no one really wanted to hear a pearl of wisdom after being given the confirmation that the man they loved was, indeed, cheating.

Be they reserved, crying or ass-kicking mad, Jessie still told women the one thing she wished she'd been told. Don't make excuses. Her fiancé had cheated on her because he was a selfish bastard. Not because of anything she did or did not do.

Jessie wouldn't invent an excuse for herself now. She'd missed crucial details tonight because *she'd* not done enough research.

"What's a Talbart?" Cole asked.

"Remember that man who hired me to 'catch' his spouse having an affair, but it turned out to be him and his wife trysting in the men's room?"

Cole nodded. "I'm guessing they like the thrill

of getting caught, but with someone they pay to keep quiet."

"Exactly. Those were the Talbarts, and they refer a lot of their friends. They don't tell me their intentions when they set up my services, that's part of their fun. Anyway, I just realized, this couple tonight is probably a Talbart referral."

She heard a giggle. The sound of a twig snapping. Cole crouched lower without having to be told. She could appreciate a man knowing when to make himself covert. Although Cole had already done his fair share of sneaking from his father back in high school.

Jessie became instantly alert. A man and woman walked into the park. She trained her binoculars, and recognized the shadowy features of the man she'd met in her office. So much for spying on his *cheating* wife. Jessie would lay cash money the woman at his side shared his last name and had a ring on her finger.

Talbarts. True, it beat actually discovery infidelity. Despite starting this business with good intentions, constantly discovering betrayal was wearing her down. She switched out of the binocular setting, adjusting her lens. She had to be prepared for the right shot to come about. There was a fine line in getting the detail she needed. Too much zoom messed up night shots.

The woman turned her head, and her smiling face came into view. Jessie almost dropped her camera.

Thank God her quick intake of breath hadn't echoed in the night.

Cole tensed beside her. "Isn't that…"

She closed her eyes for a moment. This was a disaster. "I don't know. It's too dark to tell." Okay, huge lie, because she was pretty darn sure she knew exactly who that woman was.

Jessie took a breath and let it out slowly. She'd blown it. She looked at the woman, who was holding hands and kissing the man passionately. Jessie took her shot quickly. A mistake, but she wanted to get out of there as soon as possible. To get Cole out of there.

Why in the world had she thought inviting him was a good idea? He worked in TV. The *Just Between Us* station also covered local politics. And spotting the embattled mayor of Knightsville, Georgia, canoodling in a park would be a nice little coup for his colleagues. Yeah. She'd blown it big-time.

Damn, and she actually liked Mayor Brock. She'd pushed through a lot of funding for the police force, area schools and ironically city parks.

And just when Jessie thought things couldn't get any worse, she spotted the man, sans dog, with his own camera aimed at the couple. Great.

JESSIE WALKED SILENTLY toward the car. Cole knew something was wrong. Shit. Maybe he did have his finger on the pulse of a woman's wants, or whatever the hell that article had said, because he was sensing her mood. He needed a beer.

No, it wasn't that. Any idiot would note the tenseness of her shoulders. The distance she was keeping between them reminded him of those sayings about a ten-foot pole. The soft, sexy woman who'd kissed him earlier, and whose sweet moans of pleasure had nearly brought him to his knees, was gone.

Without a word, she unlocked her car and he slid into the seat beside her. He turned to speak to her, to find out what was wrong, but she'd already jammed her key into the ignition and fired up the engine. She jerked the car out of the convenience-store parking lot as he buckled his seat belt.

Clearly here was a woman who couldn't wait to get away from him.

No, he definitely didn't have his finger on the situation, because otherwise he'd know what the hell was going on. And how to fix it.

They rode in silence back to the station, where she'd picked him up. She pulled alongside his car, and stared forward. Engine still running. He got the message.

"'Bye, Jess," he said as he stepped out. She'd turned her head as he closed the door. Their gazes met through the glass. The lights in the parking lot illuminated her beautiful face. She opened her mouth as if she wanted to say something. Her expression softened, appeared unsure, and for a moment he knew he was back on track. Then she nodded and he watched as she drove away from him.

He dug his keys out of his pocket. Women. He'd been married to one. Worked with them. Was raising two of them. But he'd never understand them.

Like the mayor tonight, she was in a fierce battle for her job. Why was she out playing night games in the park? That would be fodder for the competition and reporters alike.

He was an idiot.

Jessie's attitude had changed right after he'd recognized Mayor Brock. Jess probably thought he'd report it immediately to the news people at the station. As much as he'd like to have that kind of scoop, he'd never do that to Jessie.

The tight knot that had seized his muscles eased. This was something he could fix. He unclipped his cell phone and dialed Jessie's number.

"Hello."

Just the sound of her sexy voice made him hard.

"Jessie, I'd never use what I saw tonight in the park. That was just…us. Not my job."

She exhaled in relief. "That's good to know."

He smiled, because he heard the warmth return to her voice. Time to lay it all on the line. "I want you Jessie. I want to finish what we started."

Her breath hitched. "You know, I make my worst decisions after midnight."

"I think I heard that on some TV show." His

show. She'd said it in that interview with Eve. Cole looked at his watch. "Lucky for us, it's long past that."

Her breath came out in a soft moan. "Then why don't you stop over at my place?"

He closed the phone, anticipation making him harder. With a nod to the security guard on his rounds, he jumped into his car and started the engine.

9

THE DOORBELL RANG, and despite knowing it would be Cole, Jessie still looked through the tiny glass peephole out of habit. There he was—big, strong and impatient.

Her breath caught in her throat. Damn, but this could be awkward. Here was a man coming over to her home specifically to have sex. This wasn't a good-night kiss that led to unbelievable passion and getting carried away. This was a blunt, I'm-opening-the-door-just-to-lead-you-to-my-bed encounter. She knew it was probably a mistake. Why open herself up to pain like this? She'd been infatuated with him once. And although he probably never knew it, he'd very nearly broken her heart.

Yes, a toe-curling, can't-wait-to-make-it mistake.

And the fling rules would be there to make sure her heart didn't become involved. After all, Cole Crawford was a bad boy, so that made him the perfect candidate for a fling.

She schooled her features, trying to wipe the silly grin off her face. After taking a deep breath, she unlocked and opened the door.

Her porch light cast a yellow shadow across the planes of his face. A hint of a beard darkened his chin. He looked tired, agitated and ready. She didn't know how to play this.

With two quick strides she was in his arms. He kicked the door closed, and backed her toward the wall.

Apparently, Cole knew how to play it.

He lifted her off the ground, and she wrapped her arms around him. He propped her up against the sturdy entry table she tossed her mail and keys on. Their lips were almost even, and their mouths met. Fused. She kissed him with all the angst she'd had for him as a shy teenager, and all the hunger she had for him as an experienced woman.

Jessie reached for his shirt, wanting it off of him. She itched to stroke the smooth skin of his back. He stopped kissing her only long enough to allow her to tug the soft material over his head.

Cole pulled her T-shirt from her pants. "Why'd you tuck this back in?" His voice was rough as he slid his lips along her cheek. Licked her neck.

"So you could drag it out again."

He laughed against the pulse at the base of her neck. Gave her skin a gentle bite.

Her nipples tingled. Tightened. She ached for his touch on her breasts, and she wanted it all. His hands, his lips all over her body. Jessie wanted to rub her breasts against his chest, savor the heat and friction.

Why was he taking so long getting her shirt off? "Take it off," she urged.

Cole wasted no time. Seconds later her shirt fell to the floor. Quickly followed by her lacy black bra.

"I wore that bra just for you."

"I'll admire it later."

His lips didn't return to her. Noting their absence, she opened her eyes. Cole stood before her, gazing at her bared body. He was sucking in air, his breathing harsh. Doing nothing but staring at her breasts.

Slowly, his gaze lifted to meet hers. "You're stunning."

She almost said something flip like, "Well, in that case, look all you want." But she didn't want only his eyes on her. Jessie wanted *him* on her.

"Kiss me," she said. Her voice was low and filled with hunger.

Cole shook his head. He reached over and flipped the switch. The lamp bathed her skin in a soft, luminous glow. "So far it's only been in the dark. I want more than to just feel you."

Jessie shivered as his fingertip traced the line of her collarbone.

"I want to see you as I touch you." His fingers slid down the slope of her breast. Her nipple puckered harder. He cupped her with his hand, his thumb caressing her sensitive tip. "I want to watch that."

Her skin grew flushed from the heat of his words.

Jessie shook her hair behind her shoulders. She wanted him to see her.

"Strip for me." His voice was raw.

She saw the outline of his erection in his pants. She'd done that to him. She wanted to do even more.

His suggestive words sent a shaft of white-hot desire through Jessie's body. She slid off the table. Stripping was something she had to do standing up. Her gaze met the dark brown of his eyes. She let her fingers caress his muscular arms, then found the button of her pants. With barely a fumble, she unbuttoned and unzipped them. Cole groaned low in his throat when she shimmied out of them, letting the material slide down her hips, past her thighs to pool at her feet.

She stood before him clad only in a pair of black panties so wispy and small they were hardly a covering. Jessie hooked her thumbs around the thin strip of silk at her hips. "Watch me."

Cole's gaze lowered as she did a slow tease, sliding the material down one hip, then the other. His intake of breath was harsh, and suddenly she didn't want to tease him. She wanted that material off right then. Her panties dropped to the floor, and she kicked them aside.

Jessie reached for his hands. The rough strength of his fingers excited her, and she couldn't wait to feel his touch on her skin. With a small smile, she placed one of his hands on her breast, the other between her thighs.

His touch was more hurried this time. Less practiced. She rose on tiptoe and pressed her mouth to his at the same moment he slipped his fingers past the slick folds between her legs. She gasped against his mouth.

"Cole, that feels so good."

But she didn't want to be the only one feeling good. She wanted to touch him. *Hold* him. Make him as desperate as she felt. She tugged at the waistband of his jeans, bringing him closer. She found the button, and made quick work of the zipper. With a speed only sexual need could give her, she had those pants down around his ankles. His boxer briefs followed. Then she broke off the kiss and pushed him back.

A hungry confusion dwelled in the depths of his brown eyes.

"I want to see you, too," she said.

He took a step back to tug off his shoes, then kicked his pants and briefs aside.

Her gaze dropped, soaking up the strength of his chest, the dusting of hair. The rock-solid flatness of his stomach. His hard cock hung there firm and heavy, pointing toward her. Waiting for her. She wrapped her fingers around him. His skin was hot, and he shuddered. His hands returned to her body. She stroked the smooth head of him and he closed his eyes with a groan.

Jessie's knees grew shaky with that harsh sound from him. Who knew hearing a man's need for her would make *her* heart pound? Her body readied. The fingers between her legs moved easily now.

"Jessie," he rasped. He swallowed. "Feeling how much you want me…"

His penis hardened further in her hand, and a deep earthy satisfaction filled her. "I know," she said. Her voice was raspy and tight. She nipped at his bottom lip.

"Now," she said.

"Wait, I have to tell you something." His voice strained with control.

No, no, no. She didn't want to hear anything. Jessie almost groaned in frustration. No confessions. No admissions. She just wanted him inside her, making her feel good. Why did she always get the bad boy trying to do right by her?

His hands left her body, finding her shoulders. Jessie stared at him, feeling too raw to hide her disappointment.

"I can't think when you look at me like that."

"Then don't think," she said, but he was already shaking his head.

Cole glanced away and sucked in a breath. Then his eyes once more met hers. Serious and direct. "This is all it ever can be. I can't offer you anything but this."

Frustration almost screamed inside her. "Do I look like I want anything *but* you?"

His expression turned hard. Bitter. "I'm no good in relationships."

Her frustration lessened, but her hungry desire for him continued to burn. She appreciated his gallant gesture. Who knew men still acted like that? "Aren't you forgetting that I'm the advocate for the fling? I don't want a relationship any more than you do. Right now, all I want is your body."

His eyes narrowed, and he opened his mouth to speak. Then he hauled her up against him, his lips meeting hers. He kissed her. Kissed her hard, with all the pent-up raw emotion inside him. Obviously, Cole had his own demons to slay. And if she was going to benefit from that, so be it.

"Where's your bedroom?" he asked against her neck. The warmth of his breath sent a tingle down her body.

"Upstairs."

He broke away long enough to reach for his pants. Jessie saw him grab a handful of condom packets from his pocket. Another tingle slid right down her spine. She'd like to use each and every one of those packets.

He tossed his pants out of their way. "Take me there."

Jessie reached for his hand and drew him toward the stairs that led to the second floor. She stopped at the base of the stairwell to kiss him. He engulfed her in his arms, his lips hard and becoming so familiar on her own. Jessie spread her palms against his back, wanting to feel as much of his skin as possible. The packages of condoms dropped to the floor.

He gripped her shoulders, pushed her away. "Now," he said, as he turned her to face the stairs.

She missed the first step and fell backward. Cole reached for her. His steadying fingers on her hips balanced her against his chest. Her thighs bumped his leg muscles. Her backside tucked into him and he supported her weight. A low, carnal sound slowly ripped from him as his rock-hard erection pressed against the softness of her skin. Jessie thrilled at the sound. Loved knowing, *feeling,* how her touches made him want her more.

She wiggled, eliciting another deep groan from his chest. Once again the power she had over his body, over this big, strapping man, made her feel strong. Jessie wanted to make him feel all kinds of things at her hand. With her mouth.

His hands circled her waist and he pulled her tight to his chest, stilling her movements. "Enough," he said. His breath was a warm caress above her ear. "Your ass is perfect."

Now, she wouldn't fall, so with reluctance, she began to move from his arms and take him to her bedroom. But she already missed the solid heat of him behind her.

"No. Here," he said.

Her mouth went dry. Her memory flitting to last Thursday, when he had held her in the exact same way in the parking lot, and brought her to orgasm with his fingers.

His fingers skimmed across her waist and up her rib cage now. "I want to feel your nipples tighten when you come." He cupped her breast, and she shivered.

His other hand slid between her legs, his fingers sinking into the curls there. Touching her clit. If he'd do that now like he had done then…

Yes. It should be like this.

Cole gently pushed at her shoulders and she bent forward, her head inches from the beige carpet covering the stairs. Her left hand curled around a stairwell spindle, while the fingers of her right hand sank into the fibers of the carpet.

He left her briefly to take care of the condom, then she felt the tip of him against her. Sighed when his hand returned to her breast.

"You're so wet. So hot. Tell me you're ready, Jessie. I hope you are."

"Yes."

Cole surged into her then, filling her. The pleasure was intense. Building. She moaned as his fingers returned to touch her between her legs. "You feel so good, all of you."

Her nerves tingled from his tender pinch of her nipple, the exquisite teasing of her clit, and the expanse of his solid body covering her back, her legs. Then he began to pump, stroking her inside and out.

Jessie thrust her hips back, angling to meet his rhythm. Cole shifted and she gasped. He'd touched her at just the right place. Her muscles tightened. She sucked in a breath, then held it. Deep tremors took over her muscles, and she convulsed around his penis.

Cole quickened his pace, his fingers continuing their teasing.

She cried out and her legs grew shaky. Her orgasm raced through her. She lost all thought. Jessie only felt. She wanted to yell at him to go faster so the sensations would be more intense. She wanted to beg him to slow down so she could ride the wave of pleasure.

When her trembling stopped, he pulled himself from her body. Cole lifted her, turned her toward him.

"Hearing you come apart like that…"

She'd never been so loud. Jessie's eyes drifted open. His face was tight with strain. His eyes dark in the faint light seeping in from the hallway.

"But you didn't…"

He gave her a lazy smile. "I will. Like this."

Cole backed her up a few steps to the angled landing halfway up the stairs. He cushioned her as he pushed her down, until the soft carpet was tickling her back.

Even though he stood steps below Jessie, Cole loomed above her. The muscles of his shoulders and arms bunched in measured control. His penis jutted forward. She watched as his eyes scanned her flushed skin. She could imagine what she looked like. Her hair a scattered mess about her face. Her skin rosy from that intense orgasm.

Any other time she would have felt exposed. Uncomfortable. Even in front of a trusted lover. But she loved feeling Cole's gaze on her sated body. Loved knowing the sight of her made him hard. Brought that harsh intake of breath.

She balanced her elbows on the landing, raising herself higher. Her breasts peaked, and his eyes flared.

"Spread your legs for me."

Without hesitation she made room for him between her thighs.

Cole sank to his knees on the stair below her. He lowered his chest, bracing his weight beside her. He covered her, the hair on his chest teasing her nipples.

His eyes met hers. "Tell me you want me," he said.

"I want you." She grabbed his ass, drawing him closer. "I want all of you."

Something hot yet elusive flickered in the depths of his eyes, then vanished. "This is going to be so good." His words were a promise. Then he surged within her.

Her head dropped back. His touch felt incredible.

The stairs creaked as he thrust. Each stroke making her wetter. Bringing her closer. His rhythm wasn't as controlled this time. His breathing was harsh and coming out in pants. Yet he still found that special place inside her that positively made her come undone. He aimed for it as he stroked.

Jessie wrapped her legs around his waist, the friction against her clit almost too much.

A wave of red-hot pleasure took her over. She moaned, gasped his name, and he moved within her in earnest.

"Now, Jessie. Go now." The raw inflection of his voice urging her on was the most erotic sound she'd ever heard. Cole was a man on the edge. Barely able to control himself for her...that sent her over the brink.

She gripped him with her thighs as her orgasm exploded. Cole groaned above her, and she knew he was finding his own release.

10

JESSIE STRETCHED between the soft cotton sheets. Her body was absolutely sated. Her muscles so relaxed, she'd swear she'd never need a massage again.

But the physical fulfillment of her flesh couldn't begin to compete with the utter rightness she felt in her spirit. As if she'd been reborn with a whole new energy.

She closed her eyes and savored the feeling.

Her stomach clenched. Her muscles tensed. What the hell?

Jessie shot up in bed. Did she just think the words *utter rightness?*

She glanced down at the sleeping man beside her. So buff. So handsome.

So…so needing to be gone. She had to get him out of her bed. Out of her home. Now.

But how? His big body practically covered her mattress, and he slept the sleep of the dead. Or the recently orgasmed.

A small smile tugged at her lips. Of course, he'd given her two, so she'd cut him some slack. After catching their breath, they'd finally made it to her bedroom, where she'd collapsed without even pulling off the decorative shams.

Cole moved in his sleep, his hand snaking out to wind around her arm. He tugged, hauling her toward his side.

She let him, wrapped herself against him and inhaled deeply. She loved the smell of him. Citrusy and minty and very, very masculine. His fingers caressed her thighs. Okay, maybe he could stay a little longer.

What the hell was she thinking?

Jessie glanced at the clock. It was past five o'clock in the morning. Lying in bed in fitful sleep was not an option. She had another job later that night. Also, she wasn't taking into account the two-day trip to Memphis she still needed to pack and prep for. And at some time she'd have to work up the images she'd taken the night before in the park.

Warmth suffused her as she thought of the park. How Cole had kissed her on the merry-go-round. Caressed her on the swing. Place number two she'd boldly stated she'd never have sex—a park. Yeah, she could see the humor in it. First the parking lot, then the park. She might as well drag Cole to the library and do him in the stacks, just to firmly grind all those statements into the ground.

Hmm, that didn't sound half-bad.

But this really was bad. She must be far gone if thoughts of the municipal library were turning her on.

Jessie smoothed the hair out of her eyes. Get serious. Get up. Get dressed and get him out of there.

Flings were flings. They weren't sleepovers. Wake him up. Don't offer him coffee and never, ever give him a goodbye kiss.

She tapped his shoulder, ignoring how good his skin felt beneath her fingers. He rolled over onto his back, and she sucked in a breath. His eyelashes fanned against his skin. That shadow of his beard was even darker now. Those sexy lips of his, lips that did such naughty things to her in the night...

Sure, she wanted him out of her bed, but that didn't mean she couldn't appreciate him while he still slept. Cole was all man now. Any trace of the boy she knew was gone.

She'd thought him cute back then, and would daydream in civics class, thinking how soft his lips would be. Now those lips were rugged. His chin solid and strong. Where his cheeks were once thin they were now filled out. Just like the rest of him. Broad shoulders. Muscular arms.

All in all, a solid male package.

Jessie shook her head. No getting dreamy about him. If she wasn't careful, instead of doodling his name in her notebook, she'd be Photoshopping their pictures together. And trying to splice in images of future children. Only the technology and the tools had changed.

Now would be a good time for a dose of reality.

It was just sex. Incredible, toe-curling, snuggling-afterward sex, but just sex all the same. In fact, it probably wasn't even that good. It was the anticipation of all those years mixed in with a little high-school angst. Really, what man could hit the G-spot and the clit all on the first go-around?

Hell, the stairs cutting into her back had been damn uncomfortable.

Jessie tapped his shoulder again. He opened his eyes, which were more green than hazel now.

A slow smile spread across his face. "Good morning," he rumbled. His voice was deliciously sleepy.

"I didn't want you to be late for work," she told him.

He sat up with a start, the muscles of his stomach bunching as he moved. "What time is it?"

"Almost six."

He groaned and scrubbed his hand down his face. "Yeah, thanks."

The bed shifted under his weight and he pushed the covers aside with his leg. He stood. And she almost rethought coffee. The early morning sun barely flicked into the room, but she could clearly see his naked body. The palms of her hands had practically memorized it last night. For a few moments, she considered asking him to stay.

She reclined against the pillows, watching him through half-open eyes.

"You're not getting up?" he asked.

She shrugged. "Why? I'm enjoying the view. And I don't have to go to work for hours yet."

He smiled, apparently not the least bit perturbed that she was openly ogling his naked form. She sighed and wondered if women would ever achieve the utter lack of self-consciousness about their bodies that men possessed. Jessie certainly hoped so. In the meantime, she went to a dresser and grabbed a nightgown. She slid the purple silk over her head and stood in front of him.

"But, yes, I'll walk you downstairs. The alarm pad is there, anyway," she said with a wink.

His fingers tangled with hers, and she almost took a step back. *Settle down, settle down. It's not like he tried to kiss you goodbye.*

They walked hand in hand to the stairs. The scene of the crime. His clothes would be in the entryway. *Get him there now.* Her heart was pounding like it used to as she waited for him to study together.

But he didn't pause at the landing, and released her hand when they reached the bottom step. Jessie leaned against the wall as she watched him get into his clothes. The sound of his zipper signaled the ending to their interlude.

From there, they entered a whole new era of awkwardness. Situation number one they'd thankfully avoided. They both came.

But now they were immersed in awkward situation number two. That first goodbye after sex, which could be accomplished with...

That uncomfortable hug.

The strange zeroing in on the cheek for a quick, impersonal brush of his lips.

Or her personal nonfavorite, the halfhearted, "I'll call you."

She cut him a glance. Cole didn't appear ill at ease. In fact, he seemed darn confident as he strode toward her. Suddenly, her every nerve ending remembered the pleasure this man gave her, and wanted to experience it again. His finger was at her chin, and he lifted her face to look at him. Their gazes met. His thumb stroked her bottom lip, reawakening her senses. Her stomach tightened.

Then he turned away and walked to her front door and left.

Jessie's jaw dropped. That was it? Fling rules forbid any kind of romantic goodbye, so Jessie didn't need one. But still...

COLE POUNDED ALONG THE dirt path on his sister's farm. He should have been exhausted. After Jessie woke him, it had been nothing but one thing after another at the station. November was the important sweeps month. Doing the hard work now meant *Just Between Us* would continue attracting high numbers of viewers. The station manager could raise advertising rates. And that made station managers very happy.

Cole hadn't had time to think about Jessie. When he wasn't managing the production of the show, he was going through his answers for the interrogatories Jenna had given to the group of lottery winners. He hated filling out the paperwork. The questions put him on the defensive, but more than that, the task reminded him of all he could lose if his ex-wife heard about the money. There'd be no question of whether Amber would return. If money was involved, she'd be there.

Cole cursed under his breath and picked up his speed. The morning sun was filtering through the tall Georgia pines. The mornings were colder now, but he needed the exercise. Needed the quick pace to recharge himself.

He spent most of his weekends at his sister's place in the Georgia countryside, not too far from where they'd grown up. George was her second husband, but Annie always referred to him as the prize for putting up with her first. She'd been rewarded with a home, a great husband and a loving daughter. Janine was just one year older than his own girls. And a reason he'd kept the girls with his sister once school started.

After Amber left him, he'd tried to make it work for the three of them in the city. When school let out for summer Annie had invited the girls to the farm to keep Janine company, and he visited on the weekends. The girls thrived in the open air, taking to the slower-paced country life easily.

When school began in the fall, it just seemed

natural to keep Susan and Schyler with Annie and George. The girls had made so many new friends and each of them had a dog.

In Atlanta, he'd sold his condo and moved into a small apartment, saving every last penny so that he could buy a large enough house to bring them back home with him. It wasn't the ideal situation, but so much of it made sense, too. If the lottery money—

He cut off that train of thought, pushing himself faster. The money wasn't his. And every day more of it was gone, tied up in either legal fees or court costs. If-onlys didn't make things happen, and he'd lived with enough of Amber's dreamy speculation to last a lifetime. It was ironic that he'd almost not played the lottery. His ex-wife had soured him on any game of chance by using rent money or grocery money or even the girls' birthday money to finance one get-rich-quick scheme after another.

Alone at college and away from everything he'd ever known he'd spotted Amber shelving books in the library. They'd both been given jobs there on the work-study program to pay for tuition. She was beautiful. Blond and blue-eyed, but more than that, he'd recognized someone as broken as he'd been. At nineteen he'd wanted someone to save. He'd certainly found that in Amber. No one would ever look upon him as the hero back home in Thrasher.

His ex-wife just didn't want to be saved.

They'd been happy enough in the beginning. They

were finally away from their troubled childhoods and just living in the moment. But a person could only live life like that for so long. And Amber, ultimately, never wanted to give up the fun and games and take on real responsibility.

In the end he'd agreed to take on all her debt to get Amber out of their lives. Best decision he'd ever made. And in a lifetime of mistakes, he needed a choice that wasn't tinged by regret.

Jessie was a good choice. His body heated and he slowed his pace. The thought of her made him grow hard. He ached for her. He wanted her.

And she wanted him, too. Those sexy little moans she made as she came. The thrust of her hips because she wanted more of him. He shuddered. Damn, it felt good.

When he reached the porch, he took off his shoes, as was the custom when entering Annie's house. Opening the back door that led into the kitchen, he was met with the scents of bacon and something sweet.

"Something smells great," he said.

"There you are. I haven't even seen you—" Annie turned from rinsing an apple at the sink, her expression changing from concerned to comical. "You're smiling." Then she gasped, "Oh, my God, you've finally gotten laid."

How was he supposed to know he was smiling? "I smile," he said. Knowing he sounded defensive. Avoiding the hazel eyes so like his own.

She waved her hand as if to ward off an attack. "Hey, I think it's great you're finally back in the game."

Great sex. Great woman. It only took him a year and a half to get back in that game. And he'd hit the jackpot.

Annie pulled up a chair at the kitchen table and sat. "Tell me all about her."

No way was he going there. Besides, Annie knew Jessie. Everyone from their hometown knew the Huells. Annie would want to invite her for a visit. "It's not like that. This is not…a relationship."

Annie stopped slicing her apple and looked up at him. Her eyes narrowed. "Uh-huh. Yeah."

"It's a fling."

"Just a little rebound sex? Remember, I ended up married to my rebound man." Her face softened, her lips curving into a smile.

With George twelve years her senior, Annie hadn't even bothered to mention him to Cole, thinking the relationship was going nowhere. Just someone to make her feel good about herself again. Cole finally managed to talk to the guy on the phone just before he and Annie were about to be married in Las Vegas.

"How do you feel about her?" asked Annie.

Well, if he knew he'd have to talk about his feelings, he'd have avoided Jessie altogether.

No, he wouldn't.

The clock on the counter dinged. Annie stood.

"Muffins are ready. You lucked out, Cole. Would you tell everyone to come downstairs and wash their hands? Oh, and by the way, your girls helped me make the pancake batter, so maybe you can say something about it."

He nodded, and once again was thankful for his sister's interference in his life. Thankful, when it came to the girls, since he'd barely had a clue how to deal with tears, Barbies and dress-up princess costumes. The interference in his private life was new.

Five minutes later, they were all seated around the kitchen table, laughing at one of Schyler's stories. The youngest by three minutes, she liked to keep the family entertained. His heart swelled as he looked from Schyler to Susan. They were both blond, like their mother, but had his hazel eyes. And for two little girls who looked almost exactly alike, their personalities couldn't have been more different.

Schyler could make up stories about everything in the woods. She talked of fairies that brought dew to the leaves, what was really at the end of rainbows, and she loved to make her daddy laugh.

Susan, although certainly not shy, preferred quieter pastimes. They'd go on long hikes in the woods. She was curious about everything—from how the moss grew on one side of a tree, to cooking over a fire.

Cole took a bite of his breakfast. "Mmm, these pancakes are delicious. Did you make these, Annie?"

"I couldn't have done it without Susan and Schyler's help."

"They're really great, girls." Something green suspended in the pancake caught his eye. Then he saw a bit of blue. And red. "What's this colored stuff?"

"Sprinkles," the girls said in unison.

Annie gave him a wink. "Sprinkles make everything better."

Cole ate another bite. Tasted like a regular pancake to him. Girls were just different. Great, but still different. Half the time it was as if he were raising a completely foreign species.

Had they been boys, he would have had a better handle on how to deal with them. A son would not bring a miniature teacup filled with invisible tea for him to pretend to drink.

Cole wouldn't trade his girls for anything in this world, though. He wouldn't even trade the pain Amber had caused, if it meant they'd never have been in his life.

After breakfast cleanup, he and his girls spent the rest of the day together, hiking and looking for birds and other critters. One weekend, they'd taken the small boat out, patching several small holes first. He wanted the girls to learn how to fix things on their own. Be independent and never have to rely on anyone else. Except their daddy. They could always come to him.

He glanced down at his daughters, the best part of

his life. He wanted them prepared for the world, to be able to fight anything off, but he'd protect them, too.

Not like his own childhood. Cole had failed in giving them the kind of family life he'd wanted, but they'd always know they were loved. Not just something to be yelled at or hit.

That evening as the girls were taking a shower, and he was sitting at the kitchen table looking over some reports, Annie slipped into the chair beside him. "I know you thought I'd forget about this new woman, but I haven't."

"I didn't think you'd forget." Cole leaned back against the chair, ready for the attack, but showing no worry. His sister could be ruthless. Revealing weakness would be his first mistake.

Annie playfully kicked him under the table. "Then spill. Maybe you can invite her here next weekend to meet the girls."

"It's not like that. We've only just…met. Besides, I'm not going to parade a series of women through the girls' lives. I won't subject the kids to her until I know it's a relationship that will last."

Annie made a disgusted noise in the back of her throat. "Subject your kids to her? Make sure you use that exact phrase when you tell her. I'm sure she'll appreciate it."

"Like I said, this isn't a relationship… She didn't even want me spending the night." He'd been a little slow that morning, but after a shower and shave,

Jessie's intentions gradually became clear to him. What he thought of them wasn't.

Annie's eyes crinkled at the corners. "So you have some woman using you for sex? That's priceless. In fact, maybe it's better."

Put like that, what did he have to complain about? A sexy, desirable woman wanted to screw his brains out, and asked for nothing in return… Yeah, nothing to complain about.

His sister's face grew serious. "Mom called me again."

Cole sighed heavily. "Why can't she understand I'm not interested?"

"She's trying to make amends. Explain."

The only thing worse than being the son of Michael Crawford was being married to him. But what Cole could never understand was their mother leaving him and Annie with the man. Annie got married to the first person who'd asked, and ran as far away from Thrasher as she could. He knew his sister, though, she felt a lot of guilt about Cole being alone with their father, especially after she learned what happened. Michael had only yelled and punched holes in walls while she was living under his roof. The hitting didn't start until their father had lost his job.

Two towel-wrapped bundles scampered into the kitchen, saving him from any exploration of feelings his sister might have wanted to subject him to.

"Tell her none is needed." It was true. He didn't want any explanation from the woman now. He knew enough and could guess the rest. He just didn't want to have a relationship with her.

"Daddy, is it time to tuck you in?" He couldn't remember how their ritual had started, but he would tuck them in on Friday nights, and they always took over the task on Saturday.

"Comb out your hair and put on your pajamas and I'll be ready." His daughters darted back out of the kitchen.

Annie stood up and kissed him on the cheek. "It's good to see you back among the living. I know you know this, but not every woman is like Amber, and out there is the perfect woman for you. It may not be this one, but enjoy the moment nonetheless."

Cole watched his sister walk away. She was confirmation that big girls didn't come from fairy tales. He imagined Schyler would be like that.

Still, he knew the truth—that no perfect woman was waiting for him.

He walked to the spare bedroom Annie had allocated to him for his weekend stays. Saturday nights were quiet. All three of them would snuggle in the blue overstuffed chair in the corner, one girl on either side of him. Then they'd take turns reading him a book.

They bounded into the room and leaped onto the chair.

"Hey, wait a minute. You're on my jacket," he said.

His daughters giggled as he tossed the jacket onto the corner of the bed. Then they all settled into the chair together. Susan snuggled close to him on the right, Schyler on his left.

"What's that smell?" he asked.

"Blueberry," Schyler told him.

Susan shifted, not wanting to be left out. "Strawberry. Aunt Annie took us to the body store and let us pick out lotion with glitter in it." She stuck out a tiny arm.

Sure enough, she sparkled.

"Aunt Annie says it's important to smell like a girl. Janine got pear."

He smiled, inhaling the light scent. Wasn't bad. Apparently trips to the body store and glitter lotion had replaced the baby lotion smell of old. "Who read to me first last time?"

"Schyler did." Susan opened her book. She'd taken an interest in nonfiction, and read him a story about how tadpoles turned into frogs.

Schyler chose a story about a bear who accidentally got onto a subway.

They were growing up.

They were much more sure with the words, only occasionally needing his help. Their cute smiles were being replaced by adorable toothless grins and visits from the tooth fairy. Someday they would say they were too old to read stories to their old man. They'd stop calling him Daddy. He winced at the thought of being referred to as Dad.

The girls fell asleep in his bed. For a while he just looked at them, amazed something so remarkable could come from his disastrous marriage with Amber. He'd miss the little girls they were, but knew each new year would bring something different.

One at a time he picked the girls up and carried them to their room, carefully setting each on her bunk and pulling the sheet up around her neck.

He closed their door, a smile on his face.

Instead of heading back to his room, he opted to take a walk outside. He should have thought of nothing else but falling into his own bed. His late nights at the studio and being with Jessie had made a dent in his routine. Normally, he didn't mind the lack of sleep or hectic schedule, but something had changed. Maybe he *was* returning from someplace dark. A surge of strength coursed through his body.

For a year and a half he'd done nothing but take the days as they'd come. But no longer.

Cole was ready to make up for lost time. Make up for lost time with Jessie.

_11_

JESSIE SET DOWN HER BAGS and locked the heavy wood door of her house behind her. She strode over to the couch, practically falling on it. It was good to be home. Her trip had gone well. A company in Memphis had hired her to do extensive background checks on its employees and set up routine surveillance. Some low level thievery was going on, and her client wanted to get it identified and stopped before she'd have to report it to her supervisor. The woman had been a former customer of Jessie's.

Jessie smiled while thinking of the changes that had come over Sarah Fulton. Only six months ago she'd sat crying in Jessie's office. Jessie had caught Sarah's man on film, a guy who'd found nothing wrong with banging another woman.

Jessie's bangs ruffled with her heavy sigh. Yeah, love sucked, and she wouldn't be suckered anymore. Neither would Sarah. They'd quickly found the culprit in Sarah's division. Now she'd have a name for her supervisor, instead of just going to him for help because she couldn't find the guilty party.

Jessie took the stairs to her bedroom two at a time, ready to slide between her sheets and sleep. This was a new kind of satisfaction. Way better than an infidelity case or a couple of Talbarts, so it was a nice challenge, too. Realizing the path her thoughts had just taken, and the significance of it, she paused at the top of the stairwell. When had she stopped looking forward to investigating possible infidelities? It was what her practice was based on.

She also liked catching up with a former client. That was it. Relieved, she jumped back into motion. Once in her bedroom, she unzipped her boots, tossed them into the bottom of the closet and headed for the bathroom. She'd avoided thinking about Cole while on her trip. After all, this was only a fling, and she was long past the time in her life when she would dwell on a man. However, seeing her bed, she found that the memory of being twisted among the sheets, with Cole's hips pounding against hers, took center stage.

Okay, new rule. Flings should take place out of the bedroom. Away from anyplace familiar, for that matter. Hotels. His home. Wherever. Just not here.

She tried to ignore the twinkle in her eyes, which she spotted while standing in front of the bathroom mirror. She quickly spread some cream on her cheeks. No, she couldn't ignore the twinkle. Things were good. They were the best they'd been since she'd drop-kicked that bastard Keith out of her life. Before, even. She'd never felt such a sense of accomplishment, or purpose, not even as a police officer. That appearance on *Just Between Us* had really solidified some things in her life. Professionally, she was doing all right, but now, with the added business, she had true financial security. And great sex to boot.

She finished cleaning her face with a tissue and was about to brush her teeth when the phone rang. "Hello," she said, forgetting to check her caller ID.

"You make it back okay?"

Her breath caught. *Cole.* Despite the fact that calling to check on someone was against fling rules, Jessie felt warm all over. "Yes."

"You don't have to work a case tonight, do you?" he asked, his voice low and sexy and all ready to send a thrill down her back if she'd let it. Could Cole Crawford actually be calling her to ask if she were up for a little late-night sex?

"No, I figured I'd be too tired after the weekend."

"That's too bad. I have a case just for you."

She wound the phone cord around her finger. "Let me guess. Only I can solve it?"

He laughed softly. "Correct."

"That's a very corny line," she said, smiling.

"I'm a little rusty." Although, he sounded confident and not one bit embarrassed.

She laughed in turn, glad he didn't try to deny he was using a line on her. Somehow it made it all the more fun. "I might be up for delving into some…corruption."

"I'll be right over."

Jessie remembered her new fling rule. "No, I do my best work at the scene of the crime. Your place."

A long pause greeted her statement. "Okay," he said slowly. His voice definitely didn't have the same playful, husky tone.

She had to remain firm. Rules were rules.

"See you in an hour? You have my address?"

Relief hit her. She hadn't irritated him. "Yes on both counts. I Googled it."

Jessie heard him laugh as she replaced the receiver. She almost skipped to the bathroom. She wasn't going to worry about makeup, but she did need to put her hair back into a ponytail. Her lips twisted in a smile. Cole wanted an investigation. He'd get exactly what he was after.

She stripped off her clothes, then stood naked in front of her chest of drawers. In the back was a shocking red g-string thong and matching peekaboo bra. Her "almost was" maid of honor had given it to her shortly before Jessie's canceled wedding. Jessie had almost thrown the lingerie set away. And although she didn't really need the proof, wearing it tonight would prove to herself she'd finally left Keith, physically and mentally.

She stepped into the panties, gliding the material over her thighs. Goose bumps formed on her legs in anticipation of Cole's fingers sliding that material right back down. The bra quickly followed, and she slipped into a pair of red heels she'd bought on a lark. Every self-respecting P.I. should have at least one trench coat in her possession. When she started her business, she'd bought it and a fedora as a joke. That hat would complete her costume tonight.

Jessie should have felt silly in the outfit, instead, she felt wonderfully sexy wearing next to nothing under that coat. She raced to the car. She'd risk being early. The soft lining of the coat sensually caressed her skin. She put her foot on the gas and her car moved through the Atlanta night quickly.

Jessie pulled into a parking space in front of Cole's apartment complex and took a deep breath. He lived in not such a great area of town. She hadn't realized that when she'd jotted his address down earlier. She'd be almost nervous here alone at night, and she knew self-defense. Had she copied the address wrong?

Her heart gave a quick jump when she spotted Cole waiting for her by the iron stairs. He stood under the security light, the moths zooming above his head. He was at her car door before she had a chance to open it, his expression concerned, and maybe a little embarrassed.

"I called you back to say we should meet somewhere else, but you'd already left." The grooves beside his mouth deepened. "I've never brought anyone here before. The rent's cheap and I can save up…for the girls."

Her stomach clenched. She hated how this proud man felt he had to explain. There was a time when Cole had only had his pride, and then that had been taken by his father.

She smiled up at him. "No distracting me. I'm on a very important investigation."

"Well, I—"

The coat parted as she stood, revealing a long length of her naked leg.

Cole's expression relaxed as he helped her out of the car. His eyes narrowed as his gaze traveled across her bared skin.

"I need to inspect the scene immediately."

"It's a dangerous place."

Jessie ran her finger along his strong jawline. "I'm counting on it."

He led her toward the stairwell and ushered her inside. Cole's place didn't have a lot of furniture. There was a recliner, a TV sitting on a milk crate and a beat-up chrome kitchen table with two mismatched chairs. Clearly, he didn't bring his daughters here. He'd mentioned he never brought anyone. *Any woman,* her mind supplied. Despite being against fling rules, she liked it.

The air held a hint of piney cleaner, Cole's citrusy-mint cologne and him. She took in a deep breath and scanned the space. Investigative habits were hard to break.

The one thing that added any kind of personality to the place was the wall of pictures. They featured two little girls in various ages from babyhood to school age. The photos reminded Jessie that Cole had a life completely different from the one she knew.

That's the way it would stay. And yes, she'd ignore that strange pang in her heart.

Other than their blond hair, they favored Cole. Lucky girls. They each had an infectious grin. Had Cole been born with a different life, had a different father, would he have possessed that same spark as those little girls? She hoped so.

More pictures lined the hallway. She assumed that corridor led to his bedroom, and it was the area of his home that needed the most investigating.

"Would you like something to drink?"

No drinks. No stories. This was a fling, so picture speculation should also be out. She could, however, role-play.

She shook her head and stalked toward him, poking his shoulder. "Don't distract me from my job. Something very improper has or is about to happen in this apartment."

He lifted a brow in mock surprise, but stood his ground under her investigative threat.

Jessie took a slow walk around him, unfastening her coat. When she faced him again, she stuck her hands on her hips, giving him a full view of what she wore underneath. Which wasn't much.

Cole sucked in a breath, his gaze wild and all over her body. "I confess. Make me pay."

She laughed, then gasped as he lifted her off her feet and carried her down that mysterious hallway. He lowered her in front of the bed. Those he-man tactics were actually kind of hot. Her skin flushed. Maybe she'd let him do the macho man stuff to her later.

"Are you trying to take over my investigation?" she asked as she slid down his body and found her shaky legs once more.

His eyes darkened in the lamplight of his bedroom. This space was just as sparsely furnished as the front, but the bed with the champagne colored silk sheets looked, oh, so inviting. "I see you turned down the covers. Easier to get into bed. I like a man who thinks ahead. Silk? Quite illicit."

He stripped her of her coat and his fingertips trailed lazy patterns on her flesh. "Illicit is how they'll feel on your skin."

"Embracing your shady side, I see. Let's put it to the test. Just so you really feel like this is punishment. We'll call this game 'Let's See How Much Cole Can Take.'"

His body already showed signs that he was up for this. She yanked his shirt from his jeans, anxious to get him naked.

"I'm thinking first I'll stroke every inch of *your* skin." With her fingers, Jessie lightly traced the pattern of his muscles. She began with his chest, the hair there tickling her palms. Leaning forward, she kissed each nipple. Ran her tongue around the hard tip. Cole groaned, his hands fisting in her hair.

"I've heard some men have nipples as sensitive as a woman's. Is that true?"

"Find out," he said, his voice a groan.

She grazed him gently with her teeth, and he moaned above her ear.

She lowered her hands, running them along his ribs. She loved the way goose bumps appeared on his arms. His stomach dipped as she moved her palms along the flatness above the waist of his jeans. She grew wet at the feel of his muscles bunching as she wound a path down his body.

His hands sought her breasts. His fingers tried to slip under her red bra.

"No touching. This is *my* investigation."

Her fingers found the top button of his jeans and guided it through the hole. The bulge behind the zipper grew larger. She loved the way his body responded to her touch. She could play this game all day. But she didn't want to wait, and pulled down the zipper.

Cole disobeyed her rules, stroking her skin.

She wrapped her arms around his hips, then sank her hands down the back of his pants. She cupped that cute butt of his, loving the play of muscles again. Hooking her thumbs around the waistband of jeans and briefs, she gave a careful tug. Once free, his cock thrust forward, erect and waiting for her. He kicked his shoes and pants aside.

"I want to touch every part of you." She lowered herself to her knees. Her fingers made a wavy pattern as she slid them upward, touching his calves. His knees. His thighs. When she reached the base of his penis, she stopped. "Maybe I should just leave this part of you alone," she said. Even as she taunted him, his penis grew bigger. Harder.

"Jessie. That feels so good."

She loved teasing him this way. When had she become a tease? Cole had given her the freedom.

No. This fling had given her the freedom.

Jessie lightly traced a pattern up his cock, circling around the head, then back down again.

"Does that feel good?" she asked. Not waiting for a response, she went on. "Now I'll do the same thing, but with my lips. And my tongue."

A deep, low moan was his only answer.

Slowly she stood, rubbing her body against his. Jessie shoved at his shoulder and he fell onto the bed, taking her with him. She leaned over him, mashing her breasts against his muscled chest. The perfect fit. Stretching, she licked the sensitive skin of his wrist, then drew a line up his arm with her tongue. Only stopping when she swirled it below his ear.

With a surprising jerk of his hips, he rolled her over onto her back. He loomed above her, his intent to drive her wild clear in his eyes. So bad boys didn't just grow up to be bad men. They became very bad men. Deliciously bad.

He reached for the red straps of her bra, pushing them down her arms until her breasts were freed. Finally showing him what the material had only hinted at. The straps captured her arms at her sides, making it awkward for her to move. Had he done that on purpose?

His mouth sought her breasts, drawing the tips into its wet warmth. She forgot all about wanting her hands free, because what he was doing to her felt amazing.

"You're the sexiest woman," he said against her skin. His words and warm breath sent shivers through her body. "I almost dragged you down to the floor in there when I saw those red panties."

His lips followed the line of her rib cage and lower. He circled her navel with his tongue, then traced the red thong with his mouth. The softness of his lips shooting desire through her. She wanted him. Craved him.

"I want these off you now."

She couldn't agree more. "Yes," she said.

Cole didn't waste a moment, nipping the elastic of her panties between his teeth and dragging them down her thigh. He switched to the other side, his lips at her hip. She sucked in a breath when she felt the gentle graze of his teeth on her skin. Then at the thin material. Then nothing. She raised her pelvis to meet him.

With a deep chuckle, he wound his fingers around

the small triangle between her thighs and pulled the panties out of his way. His fingers a caress against the sensitive skin of her thigh, her inner knee, her ankle. "Leave your shoes on."

Jessie's eyes met the hunger burning in his.

"I want you with those shoes on and nothing else."

She shivered. Something about his request made her feel utterly decadent.

She lifted herself up on her elbows. "Wait a minute. How did I end up flat on my back? I'm supposed to be doing the interrogation. I see I'll have to take more forceful measures."

Jessie rolled out from under Cole, pushing him to the bed with a playful shove. After drawing the belt from her coat, she reached for his wrist. Her breasts were even with his lips and he kissed her.

"Try all you like, I won't be dissuaded," she told him as she loosely tied one loop of the belt around his left arm. "But keep at it."

He circled the tip with his tongue, making her gasp. She tied his right arm with the other end of the belt. "That should keep your hands to yourself."

Then she straddled him. Although they were both in a playful mood, she paused for a moment. Closing her eyes at the pleasure. The hardness of him against the slick heat between her legs.

"I want you now," he demanded.

Jessie made a tsking sound. "So soon? I haven't explored all your best parts with my mouth yet."

Cole moved his hips, positioning himself closer to the wetness of her body, sending a tiny shock through her. "In agony, are you?" she asked, feeling a little of that agony herself.

She slowly reached for the condom she'd left in her coat pocket, drawing out his wait, drawing out his tension. Jessie wanted him aching for her. Like she was for him. Her nipples were needy. Her clit throbbed for his touch. Inside, she was slick and ready for him.

"Here's my first clue. What should I do with it?" she asked as she moved against him. So wet he slid easily against her.

"Jessie," he growled, "I will get my revenge."

A thrill of erotic sensation pooled between her legs. This game was fun and something she'd fantasized about on those long, boring stakeouts. He was in the TV business. Did his fantasies involve lights? Maybe a camera?

She moved away from him as she opened the package, then rolled the latex down the long, hard length of him. He groaned when she got to the base of his cock.

"Untie my hands." His voice was a command. As an officer, she'd always followed orders. As a fiancée, she'd always complied with her man's requests. As a lover…not so much.

"I don't think so. I like you like this. And I like playing the bad girl too much," she told him, as she straddled his hips once more. Jessie reached for him, teasing herself with the tip of his erection. His soft, smooth head shooting a thrill through her.

Cole lifted his hips, seeking entrance. "Ride me, Jessie."

The carnal urging in his voice made every pulse point ache to have him inside her. Jessie lowered herself on him. They both groaned when he was fully seated inside her.

"Ride me hard," he instructed. His eyes were closed, his jaw set. His voice, his whole body testified to the strain he felt.

Jessie was desperate to comply with what he implored in that deep, sexy voice. He was temptation. She lifted from him, only to slam down over and over again on his cock. Her movements became more frantic, more urgent. He surged higher into her, hitting every spot that made her writhe.

Suddenly, her inner muscles gripped and held him. Wave after wave of heat assailed her most intimate parts. Cole tensed below her. His big body shook as he pounded up into her and came with a roar.

She collapsed against him, her every muscle weak. The heaviness of their breathing filled the bedroom.

He pressed a light kiss to her temple. "I've never experienced anything like that." He sounded awed. Reverent.

She lifted her head and looked down into his eyes. "Maybe you should give up control more often," she teased, her voice all erotic suggestion.

"Who said anything about me losing control? As I recall, I had to take over with the strokes there at the end."

12

JESSIE SLID TO COLE'S side and snuggled against the long length of him. Breathing in his minty citrus scent. He also smelled a lot like her, which brought a smile to her face. Since she was determined to keep this thing between them a fling, she should probably be thinking of leaving right now.

"You going to keep me tied up like this?" he asked.

She laughed, brought his arms from above his head and untied the belt from his wrists. The knots were pretty loose. Jessie gave him a narrowed look. "I think you could have gotten out of those puny restraints yourself."

He winked, his eyes fully hazel now. "Seemed important for you to keep me hemmed in."

She shifted away. Jessie couldn't meet his gaze. He was right. *She* wanted to be in control. She needed to have the power. There wasn't even any pretending that they were on some kind of equal level when in bed. Certainly, they hadn't been a few moments ago.

Cole's fingers sank into her hair, and he maneuvered her head so it rested on his shoulder. She relaxed against him, still lost in thought. Cole hadn't even cared she wanted to be the dominant partner in bed. Based on the satisfied look on his face, he'd reveled in her feminine power.

He stretched and switched the bedside light off, plunging the room into darkness.

Okay, apparently she was supposed to sleep with him, which officially violated the first rule of a fling. No sleepovers. Yet lethargy pulled at her muscles. Cole's deep breathing lulled her into joining him. She was a night person. She did her best work after eleven. It couldn't be much later than that now. She shouldn't desire sleep.

Of course, she had exerted a lot of energy. His warmth was so tempting. She'd allow herself a quick nap. A power nap. In fact, she'd wake up, then awaken Cole. This closing her eyes made a lot of sense.

But the sun woke her up. With a quick start, she rolled over. Cole was on his side, facing her. Playing with a strand of her hair. His expression thoughtful. He was bright and shiny and very, very good to see in the morning.

She squinted, and her breath came out in a laugh. "Did you dress up special for me?"

He met her eyes, looking confused. "What?"

"You realize you're covered in glitter, right?"

Cole sat up, and his fingers immediately went to the short dark strands of his hair. His feet hit the floor, and he stalked to the bathroom, careless of his nudity. But then, his particular brand of nudity was incredible. The daylight played along the strong muscles of his back, his ass, firm and round, as he walked.

Jessie picked up his discarded T-shirt from the floor, and flipped it right side out. She took a moment to breathe in his scent, then pulled it over her head. That kind of intimacy wasn't forbidden by the fling rules, although it probably should be. Her heartbeat quickened. She followed him to the bathroom, and leaned against the wall. A smile tugged at her lips as she watched him examine his hair in the mirror.

"It's the girls. My sister bought them glitter lotion. They both jumped on my jacket. Some of it must have rubbed onto my hair."

"It looks fantastic."

He turned and faced her. "Don't laugh, you have it all over you now."

"Ha. I'm a girl. I'm supposed to have it on me."

His eyes trailed down her form. Her nipples hardened, poking at the thin material of the T-shirt. His gaze coasted lower still, pausing where his shirt ended at the top of her thighs. Her skin warmed under his gaze.

Then his eyes met hers. "You're some girl."

The way he said it. His words stretched out and low. As if he relished how much a girl she was. Keith had always made her feel stupid. *You run like a girl.*

Are you going to cry now? Stop being such a girl.
Hell, she *was* stupid to have stayed with such a jerk
for so long.

Tonight, she'd jog like a girl. She'd do girl push-
ups. She might wear some glitter.

She wanted to laugh at how good she felt.

*You're supposed to be with someone who makes
you feel good. Not bad.*

Her father had told her that. Somewhere along the
line she'd forgotten it. Now she recognized it as one
of the best pieces of advice he'd ever given her. She
wouldn't forget it again.

She'd wanted the kind of marriage her parents
had. Maybe they spoiled her. Thirty-five years and
they were still in love. Jessie thought she'd chosen
someone like her father. A police officer just like her
dad, but she'd been so wrong. Strange how Mr. Out-
wardly Upstanding turned out to be a jerk, while the
bad boy had apparently grown up into a man a
woman could count on.

Cole made her feel better about herself. She
finally felt healed from the pain Keith had caused in
her life. Oh, she'd have gotten to this point all on her
own. Cole had just sped it up a bit with the way he
gave to her.

He didn't always have to be the one in charge.
With the darkening of his eyes, and the sexy sounds
he made when she became assertive between the
sheets…that was all the encouragement she needed.

Cole was a man who appreciated her, and that made him very, very sexy.

Her throat tightened. Tears began to form in her eyes. Girlie tears.

Who the hell cared?

Except flings didn't involve emotions. She'd have a celebratory cry in private. She glanced around the bathroom, eyeing anything that would distract her focus from crying.

On his sink counter she spotted his cologne. "That's what it is. You wear Valorous." She lifted the top and inhaled deeply. The scent made her toes curl against the cold linoleum of his bathroom floor. "It's like an orange that brushed its teeth."

"Good. That was exactly what I was going for." Cole appeared disgruntled as he took the bottle and lid from her fingers and replaced them at the back of the sink.

He turned the spigot of the shower, then faced her. "Anyone ever tell you the male ego is a fragile thing? I think I can only handle one macho image knock-down a day. I've already had two, and I've not even had coffee."

Jessie examined his face. He didn't really seem embarrassed or even annoyed, just a little…let down.

He reached around and shut the door behind her, allowing the room to heat from the warming water. Soon steam began to rise above the shower stall.

She'd made him feel bad.

Cole had given her so much that was good last night. And this morning she hadn't returned the favor. Her pulse almost hummed because she wanted to make Cole feel very, very good.

He rolled the shower door back, stepping underneath the spray.

"Cole."

His name on her lips stopped him from closing the glass door. His hazel eyes met hers. Waiting. He did want something from her.

"I think…I think you're the most stunning man I've ever seen." Her voice sounded shaky but full of truth.

Something flickered in his eyes. Something she didn't want to see. Didn't want to acknowledge. They had a history. One they'd both been avoiding. Hiding behind a fling would mask the intimacy building between them for only so long. Getting naked in front of him now, in the daylight and when reason and clear thought was the order of the day would be a mistake.

Then he held out his hand toward her. "Prove it," he said.

She swallowed and glanced down at the strong fingers reaching for her hand. For her.

What was she, crazy? Jessie crossed her arms and all but tore that shirt up and over her head. She took his hand, allowing him to pull her beneath the warm water beside him. He slid the glass door into place.

The water poured over her head as his lips descended to hers. She'd be happy to prove how beautiful she found his body.

AFTER SPENDING WAY TOO much delicious time in the shower, Cole had to rush off to work. He'd told Jessie to stay as long as she needed, then lock up. After finding his robe on a hook in the bathroom, she strolled around his apartment. She wanted to let her hair dry naturally. Since Cole didn't possess anything even remotely resembling conditioner, she wanted to avoid the dryer.

She had absolutely no qualms about looking through his personal items. She followed vampire rules, and Cole *had* invited her in. Plus, she was a private investigator. He should know she'd snoop. Hell, that was probably why he'd told her to stay. On some level, he *wanted* her to snoop. At least that's what she told herself.

Her fingers trailed along the kitchen countertop as she debated which drawer to pull open and which cabinet to sneak a peek inside. But then, who hid stuff in their kitchen? The bedroom. The bedroom was where all the best stuff was concealed. Jessie pivoted on her heel and headed in the direction Cole had carried her last night.

She didn't have many choices. Beat-up nightstand. Old garage-sale chest of drawers. Nothing appealed. Nothing spoke to her. Her heart just wasn't in it.

After unlooping the belt, Jessie flung his robe off her as fast as she could. She had to get out of here. Her heart wasn't into being nosy? What was wrong with her?

She found her red panties wadded up by the bed, her bra nearby. She had them on in seconds. Thrusting her arms through the sleeves of the trench coat took only moments. With hopping steps, she slipped into her shoes on the way out the door.

It wasn't until she was halfway to her house that she remembered her hat. Oh, well.

Once she was at her own place, she quickly donned her routine work attire, and instantly felt more herself. She reconciled her books on Mondays. Making sure clients were billed and no payments had been missed.

Jessie ran her finger down the column, pausing at the name of Brock.

Something niggled at the back of her mind. Their check had cleared. Nothing seemed out of sorts.

It was the incident at the park. The other photographer.

Although, maybe she was being paranoid? Mr. Brock had hired her under the pretense of an infidelity investigation, but the two were married. Some people liked to spice up their sex life with a little public lovemaking. Others liked to photograph or film their intimacy. The Brocks apparently liked to combine both. Just like the Talbarts.

She was paid to take photos of the Brocks in the park, not to investigate their lives. Still, something wasn't right. She reached for their file and found their phone number. Voice mail.

Jessie hung up without leaving a message. What was she supposed to say? "Anything else weird going on in your lives besides making whoopee in public places?" No way. But being an investigator, would she take another route to find out the answers she sought? No. They'd paid her for her services. These services were rendered. Case closed.

She closed the file and returned it to the cabinet.

By the afternoon, her accounts were settled and she'd confirmed all standing appointments. If business continued on this level, she could hire an administrative assistant. That would be a huge help.

Her phone rang and Jessie answered it while shutting down her computer. "Huell Investigations."

"Hi."

Cole. Despite her warning her body not to, it reacted. Her heartbeat quickened and her neck flushed.

"Hey," she said. Brilliant, scintillating conversation. She toyed with the strand of hair he'd played with earlier.

"What are you doing?"

"Some paperwork."

"Do you have a stakeout tonight?"

She eyed her printed schedule. "No, but I do for the rest of the week."

"We just closed the show for the day. It was a good one."

Jessie shook her head. What was going on here? This back and forth between them…it seemed suspiciously like a conversation.

"Why are you calling me?" she asked.

He took a moment before answering her. "What do you mean why am I calling you? I wanted to talk to you. I thought about you all day."

Despite the thrill his words gave her, they also set off an alarm.

"You can't," she exclaimed, sounding way more desperate than she should. "I mean, this is a fling. I thought you understood. We don't call. We don't socialize."

"Fling, yes. Used for sex, no." He sighed heavily into the phone, a sound full of frustration. "Look, Jessie. Have dinner with me. I have to eat. You have to eat. Let's do it together."

She couldn't help herself; she smiled. Put like that, it did sound pretty cold-hearted. Her desperation faded. He wasn't rejecting the fling. Wasn't pushing for more. Not really. "Sure."

"I'll pick you up."

Even though he couldn't see her, she shook her head. Fling rules. "I'll meet you there."

COLE HUNG UP THE PHONE and leaned back in his chair. That call hadn't happened at all the way he'd expected it to. He'd left a laughing, sated and sexy Jessie this morning, only to meet up with Fling-Rule Huell again this afternoon.

Hell, he hadn't wanted to leave her. Judging from the greeting he'd gotten from her now, she was glad he'd finally left his own apartment.

So the woman wanted him for sex? She didn't want him to call her. Take her out to dinner. Just sex and only sex.

He guessed he should be jumping for joy. Weren't men supposed to want no-strings, no-commitment action between the sheets?

Maybe some part of him did. But not with Jessie Huell. Never with Jessie. The woman—the girl that she'd been—had saved his life.

One thing Cole knew was to never look back. He'd learned that lesson the hard way the year he'd turned seventeen. The year his dad died after one drunken rage too many and accidentally set the house on fire. The year his dad's bitterness and anger boiled over and he almost killed Cole. He never looked back, but something drew him to that time now. Probably his rekindling of his relationship with Jessie. Or maybe it was just that it was time.

Rekindling wasn't really the right word for it. The relationship between them had never been allowed to spark. He'd never allowed it. Growing up in Thrasher, Jessie was the only person in that town who looked at him with eyes not filled with contempt. Or even worse, pity. She didn't see a grease monkey or the town trash, and he loved her for it.

He sighed and scrubbed his hands down his face. He would have been blind not to know that the fifteen-year-old Jessie was infatuated with him. He'd reveled in it, the daughter of the Chief of Police, Thrasher's good girl and he could have had her anytime he wanted.

Then she passed him that note. SOMEDAY. With that one word she'd given him something. Hope, and the knowledge that Jessie Huell was special.

He sat up in his chair and fingered a stapled stack of papers on the corner of his desk. What if he'd never become off-limits because of his actions on that night? What if he'd never met his ex-wife?

Then he wouldn't have his girls.

Cole tossed the papers aside. This was the reason he didn't delve into what ifs. And didn't question the past.

He *had* involved Jessie. He *had* turned away from her. He *had* married Amber.

Amber. Even after the wringer Cole's wife had put him through, he felt guilty about the relief he'd gotten when she finally left. He'd kept the twins with him. And made plenty of mistakes there. But he never looked back—he didn't have the time. His nights and days had been spent earning a living, trying to take care of his daughters, ensuring they had a better childhood than his. That he was a better dad than his. The way to do it had been to cut himself off from anything or anyone that took him away from that focus. And he'd never looked back.

But with Jessie, he'd changed. He cared about her. Why? What made her special to him? It was the first time he'd cared about anything other than his girls and his sister's family in a long time. That felt good. His mind began to drift to the past. To when he and Jessie were growing up. Before he'd gotten distracted, made so many bad choices.

Could he lead two separate lives? Be a father who adored his daughters, who'd kill himself at work to make sure they had everything they deserved. But also be a man who snatched a few hours of pleasure with a woman he liked and whose sassy mouth drove him wild? After all the mistakes, all the hurt he'd caused…should he even try?

One thing was for sure, before he saw Fling-Rule Huell again, he needed to even the playing field.

Reaching for the phone, he punched in Penny's extension. "Do you have the taping we did on rules for a fling? The one with Jessie Huell? I'd like to watch it again."

COLE WAS ALREADY WAITING FOR HER in the restaurant when she arrived. The man had great taste. Sardella's was one of her favorite Italian eateries. The plastered mural walls depicting rural settings and the brick fireplace made her yearn for a trip to the Italian countryside. Glass-encased white tapers illuminated each red-and-white-checked tablecloth. The perfect *atmosfera Italia.* He rose when he spotted her.

Jessie's breath hitched in her chest. She'd seen this man naked, in jeans and a T-shirt and business casual. Every way he appeared made her hormones tap-dance.

She ambled to the table, taking her time so she could tell her hormones to settle down. Cole pulled out her chair.

Jessie looked up and smiled. He kissed her cheek, but his hand left the chair to cup her bottom. Reminding her just how well he knew her body.

And how well her body liked his knowing.

She pushed at his hand. "Someone will see you," she said with a laugh.

"No, they won't."

Her bad boy. She felt off balance. Cole looked so cool and in control while she felt all crazy inside. She wanted him off balance, as well.

He sat across from her, not picking up the menu.

She leaned forward. "So, when did you plan to tell me you were one of the lottery group winners?"

His water glass stopped midway to his mouth. His eyes narrowed as he met her gaze. "At first, I thought you knew."

That was one of the things she liked about Cole. He didn't try to make up some excuse or appear surprised.

"I even joked about it at the table with everyone that first night we went out."

"That's what I thought it was—a joke. Lots of people make jokes about the lottery."

Cole shrugged. "Then I figured I didn't want to tell you."

Okay, more honesty. She liked that, too. Their waiter came, poured them some red wine and took their orders.

Once he was out of earshot, she leaned toward Cole again. "Were you afraid I might only want you for your money?" she asked, her voice teasing, because clearly she only wanted him for his body.

But Cole didn't smile. He didn't even seem to see the humor in her joke. Somehow, she'd blundered, and stumbled upon his one major uncomfortable issue. But what exactly had she said? Something about wanting someone only for his money. A woman would be crazy not to want Cole for the man he was, with or without a fortune. As far as she knew, the only woman who didn't want him was…his ex-wife. The beautiful Amber Crawford.

Cole and Jessie were supposed to be having a fling. There were no personal talks in a fling. Well, hell, for that matter, there weren't supposed to be any phone calls or sleepovers, either. Since she'd broken all three rules, she might as well add long drawn-out conversations for the superfecta.

Besides, she'd been curious about the woman ever since he'd brought Amber to their hometown.

Jessie had been looking forward to that long Christmas break he'd have from college. She'd finally rounded up the nerve to ask *him* out. But all was lost when she saw how beautiful Amber was. How happy she seemed to make Cole. Resigned, Jessie placed Cole in that corner of her heart reserved for completely unattainable men. After hearing he'd had twins, she never sought information about him again, and thankfully, he had no reason to return to Thrasher so they never saw one another.

After taking a long sip of her wine, Jessie met his gaze. She dreaded her next question. Dreaded his answer. "Would the money bring her back?"

He nodded. "Without a doubt."

"Do you want her back?"

"No."

Cole didn't elaborate. Jessie liked that. He'd just given her a simple answer. But his flat tone carried a lot of emotion. No way in hell did he want to be reacquainted with his ex-wife. A warmth that didn't have anything to do with desire, or the ache she felt for Cole, settled within Jessie.

He reached across the table for her hand. "All I'm interested in right now is a hotshot private investigator."

Jessie liked that even more.

"When we were growing up, I thought you were almost too good to be true. Sweet. Smart. You know,

I wasn't really as bad in Latin as I led you to believe."
He raised his wineglass. *"Nunc est bibendum."*

Now is the time to drink.

Jessie laughed. She didn't remember a lot of
Latin, but the phrases that involved silliness, drink-
ing or sex seemed to have stuck. "So how come you
never made a move on me?" she asked.

His shoulders tensed and his gaze fell away. "Because I promised your father."

13

"WHAT? You actually made a promise to my dad? Why would you do something like that?"

"He asked me to." Cole's voice was firm and uncompromising.

Jessie dropped her gaze and took a deep breath. She didn't want him to see what she was feeling. She was so angry she doubted she'd be able to hide the emotion from her eyes. Outrage and hurt and a myriad of other feelings assaulted her. Her own father…

He'd known. Her father had known she was in love with Cole. She'd begged her dad to help him.

And then, all these years later, not a word. He'd had plenty of opportunities. The holidays she returned home for, the weekends he'd spent with her in Atlanta. If he'd told her she might have tried harder. Tried to convince Cole she was the person he was supposed to end up with. Not Amber.

Maybe that was what her father was afraid of. But why? No one could be prouder of the man Cole had become other than her dad.

Her throat tightened, but she would not lose it in

the restaurant. No matter what. She reached for her water glass. No way would she be able to handle the wine right now.

"Why?" she asked after a moment. Glad her voice sounded strong.

Cole's breath came out in a slow exhalation, as if he was gradually returning to the past. "Jessie, remember that time. Remember me at that time. I was so angry. I'd hit rock bottom, dropping out of school, stealing. Anything to get away from my dad, from Thrasher and what people thought of me there."

"No one thought any worse of you because of your dad."

Cole scoffed. "That's what I've always liked about you, Jessie. You only see the good in people. And I used that. I used you as my lifeline when the last person you should ever have been involved with was me. What would have happened if my father hadn't died? If he'd come after me when I was with you?"

Cole shuddered.

She sensed the anger he directed at himself. His frustration emanating from the rigid way he held his shoulders.

"I knew it wasn't right, but I did it anyway. Your father knew what I was doing, too, and he asked me to give you a chance at a life that didn't include the man I used to be." Cole shrugged. "So I did."

She opened her mouth, but Cole cut her off.

"Please let me tell you this. We never discussed that night, and maybe it's a conversation we should have had a long time ago."

She could easily walk away. She'd driven her own car, she wasn't dependent on him for a ride home. But she knew she wouldn't. *Now* was the time. She'd avoided this conversation that first night they'd reconnected. Had avoided this talk ever since. But now was the time.

"I have daughters. I understand now where your father was coming from. What had I grown up with? A father who used his son for a punching bag. No man wants to see his daughter with a man like that. Not until he can prove he won't follow in his father's footsteps."

She hated Cole's father, Michael Crawford, with everything she had inside her. Then and now. The man had nearly broken his son's spirit. And when Cole had fought back, Michael had almost killed him.

"Tell me about that night. What happened before you found me at the library?" Her throat felt dry as she asked the question.

The waiter came, placed their Caesar salads before them, and Cole dropped her hand. "Pepper or parmesan cheese?"

"Just the cheese," she said, trying to get the waiter to move along. She stole a glance in Cole's direction.

His face was tight and his eyes dark. He appeared to be far, far away. How ironic that they'd be having this talk now, in the impersonal atmosphere of a restaurant.

Then she realized this might be the best place for it. Surrounded by other diners, the low ambient music, the air filled with the wonderful smells of good food… Somehow it took the intensity out of the reality of the past. Made the emotions not so fierce, the pain not so piercing.

Their waiter walked on, and Cole picked up his fork. Twirled the utensil in his fingers, but made no move to spear anything in his salad.

"My father was always a yeller. That's why I never suggested we study at my house. But when Annie moved to Atlanta, things got bad." He swallowed hard. "No one will ever lay a hand on one of my daughters."

Jessie nodded. She understood. The vehemence in Cole's voice when he spoke about no one hurting his children said it all. Every little girl should be so lucky to have a father like Cole.

How could Amber have driven him away?

"I was seventeen and determined to be a man. I'd had enough."

Jessie wanted to touch him. To wrap her arm around Cole's shoulder, but knew that wouldn't be the right thing to do. She got the feeling he'd kept this story buried deep inside him. Had never discussed it with anyone, at least not in a long time. She wondered if even her father knew all the details.

She almost felt honored that he wanted to share it with her.

The fork clanged as it hit his salad plate. He left it there and raised his gaze. Such agony lay in the hazel depths of his eyes. Her stomach clenched. The pain surrounding him almost made her hurt physically.

"I shoved him. Hard. It felt good. I told him if he ever laid a hand on me again, he'd regret it."

She'd known Cole's childhood was bad, that his dad took out a lot on him, it had been hard for her to comprehend at the time. She'd grown up surrounded by love. A mother and a father who would do anything for her. Jessie vowed she'd visit them in Thrasher her next free weekend. Since starting her firm, her trips had trickled to almost nothing, and she missed them.

"I went to work at the garage, but when I got back he came after me. You saw me. I was a mess." A humorless smile touched his lips.

He'd never shown up for their Latin session. Feeling dejected, she'd started walking home. He'd pulled up beside her in an unknown car as she crossed in front of the library.

She'd cried out when she saw his face. A broken jaw. Eye socket. Nose. Then she'd cried in earnest after she climbed into the car beside him and tried to clean the blood from him as best she could. He'd asked for money. That's all he'd wanted. Some money, the car and to get away.

"No, Cole. You can't run. If you run, you'll never be able to stop running." How she knew the truth of that at age fifteen, she'd never understand, but Cole would not be the man he was today if he'd left town that night.

He'd stolen a car from the garage where he worked. Sideswiped another as he tried to get out of town.

A shudder had run through his slight frame. The boy in him had wanted to take off and hide. She could see that the man he was becoming knew she was right. She'd begged him to go to her dad.

Jessie never knew what her sheriff father had said to Cole, but after he was discharged from the hospital, he went away for months. He came back shortly before his senior year, a different person. While no scars marked his body, he'd changed. Cole had worked hard during the day, and even harder at night, to pay for the two cars he'd damaged. He'd scored high on his SAT, enough to go to college on a scholarship.

Everyone in town knew of the beatings Cole's father gave him. Of Micheal Crawford's drunken rampage that resulted in his death. Of Cole's night in jail, but Cole kept his head high.

"Do you ever think of your father?"

Cole shook his head. "Sometimes I wonder what it would have been like if he'd made it out of the house before the roof collapsed. Maybe prison would have straightened him and he'd have gotten his life on track."

She nodded, but couldn't fathom why he'd want good things for the man. But then, she imagined it was hard to stop loving a parent. "You remember that phrase I wrote one time at the diner?"

He nodded. "Yes. 'Someday.' Believe me when I tell you, sometimes that's all I had."

They finished their meal in quiet conversation. No more talk about the past. Her chicken Vesuvio had been cooked to perfection, and while at first she thought it doubtful she'd enjoy her meal, a relief that they'd finally cleared the air between them settled over their table. They didn't have dessert or even coffee. Instead, Cole took her hand and walked her to her car.

She'd placed her hand in his before. Numerous times, as he led her into the shower or helped her to stand. But this touch was different. Intimate. Intimate because of the secrets Cole had shared. At her car, he cupped her cheeks. His gaze scanned her face, then he kissed her. A light brush of his mouth along her lips. Her cheeks. Her eyes.

"Come away with me this weekend. To the cabin. I want to show you where I went that summer."

She struggled to open her eyes. She met his stare. Seeing something vulnerable in his eyes. "What about the girls?"

"Girl Scout weekend. Their whole troop is going camping. Janine and Annie, too."

"I'd like that." Jessie was surprised she'd agree to this. Surprised because she was actually looking forward to it.

But then, Cole hadn't told her the whole story. There were still pieces missing.

She drove home trying not to castigate herself. Tonight she'd probably broken every fling rule there was, and without the said benefit of the fling. Sex.

THE BROCKS WERE WAITING for her Tuesday morning outside the storefront of her official office. She'd been wrong to ignore that niggling sensation about their case. Something *was* wrong. Their tight faces and tense body language gave it away.

"Good morning," she said, as she unlocked the door and ushered them inside.

"For you, maybe." Mr. Brock's tone was scornful and angry.

Mayor Brock placed a gentle hand on his arm. "Don't antagonize her further, Tom."

Antagonize? Further?

Jessie flipped on a few lights, which illuminated the seating area of two brown leather couches, and a few chairs. Magazines were neatly piled on a pair of small end tables. Her inner office was more formal. A desk, computer and executive chairs. She invited them to take a seat on the couch there, thinking that might put them more at ease.

Mr. Brock indicated he had no intention of sitting.

"How could you do this to us? We trusted you, Ms. Huell. You came highly recommended."

"I don't know what you're talking about."

His breath came out in a hiss. "The pictures. The threats of going to the media. What is it? Are you trying to ruin my wife or just get money?"

She'd been a P.I. long enough to not let the accusations of emotionally upset people bother her. Her goal was to project a wall of calm, hoping to infuse that into her client. "I'm telling you again, Mr. Brock, I don't know what you're talking about."

A long silence greeted her statement. Finally, Mayor Brock sighed. "Tom, I don't think she does know."

Mr. Brock sank down on the couch beside his wife, his head in his hands. "What are we going to do?"

"Why don't I make us some coffee and you can tell me what is going on."

Mayor Brock nodded, and Jessie left them to prepare the coffee. The couple needed a few moments without her presence. From what she could piece together, they were being blackmailed. The other photographer… She'd known something was wrong that night.

Jessie shook her head. What she had going on with Cole had made her sloppy. She was never sloppy. After filling the bin with water, she turned the coffeemaker on and returned to her inner office. The Brocks were talking quietly, their bodies a study in anxiety and worry.

"The coffee should be ready in just a few minutes. I take it someone is trying to blackmail you?"

Mrs. Brock met her gaze. Worried, but still collected. "Yes, with pictures from that night at the park. The same night you, uh—"

Jessie nodded. "I understand. Do you have the pictures with you?"

Mr. Brock removed an envelope from his briefcase and handed it to her. Jessie examined the envelope. No return address. Postmark was Peachtree City, but that was only a quick drive from Atlanta, so no real clue there. The envelope had obviously been handled so much she doubted there'd be any usable fingerprints.

Maybe she'd get something from the pictures. She flipped through the shots, examining them closely. There were four photos. The first had the couple in a very passionate embrace. The second clearly showed Mr. Brock cupping Mayor Brock's exposed breast. The third had her hand down her husband's pants. The last showed them against the slide, obviously intimate. Each photo captured both their faces and that it was happening at a very public place after hours.

Not good.

"Anything?" Mayor Brock asked, her tone filled with a kind of resigned hope. As if she knew nothing would come of Jessie's examination, but she'd love to be pleasantly surprised.

"The quality of the black-and-white photos is quite poor. An amateur."

Mr. Brock sighed in relief.

"That doesn't mean he might not have the skills to pull off a successful blackmail." Jessie's tone was cautious. "Let me ask you something. What you did in the park—that wasn't new, was it? That's something you do on a regular basis."

"I wouldn't say *regular* basis," Mrs. Brock answered, hedging like a true politician. Jessie kept her smile to herself.

"But someone who followed you regularly…they wouldn't be surprised if you suddenly detoured to a deserted park after midnight."

The mayor dropped her gaze. "No."

"I did see something unusual in the park that night. I took a photo of a man who was also taking pictures of you."

Mr. Brock stood. "Why didn't you say something before now?"

"At the time, I wasn't sure if he was another private investigator you'd hired to find you. I have the pictures downloaded on my computer. Let's see if you recognize him."

ON WEDNESDAY, Cole donned a suit and tie. He hadn't worn such formal attire in a long time. Maybe since he'd interviewed for the job at the station five years ago. Now he stood outside a courtroom with the rest of the lottery group. Eve and Jane were talking together quietly. Zach had acknowledged him with a nod. Nicole was on her cell phone.

He couldn't believe they'd actually made it to this point. He'd never thought the lottery controversy would go this far. But there she was, Liza Skinner, standing near the doorway, her expression defiant.

How had it come to this? They'd been more than just coworkers once. Liza had been with them since the first days of *Just Between Us,* when they'd only brought in people they could trust, who were creative and didn't mind spending sixty hours a week getting an untried program on the air. As the show's first story-segment producer she'd been there to help mold the show into the success it was today. They'd been friends once. Jane and Eve had been Liza's best friends.

Jenna Hamilton, their lawyer, walked toward their small group, looking tense but efficient. Tense was good. It meant she knew they had a lot to lose and wouldn't get cocky. She acknowledged Liza's lawyer with a quick nod. He nodded back, his gaze hesitating a little too long on Jenna's chest.

Now that made for an interesting development. Cole wondered what Jessie might have thought of it. She read people well.

Images of her kept popping into his mind. Not a bad thing, he acknowledged. Just new and different— the way she'd break in on his everyday thoughts.

The bailiff opened the ornately carved double

doors that led to the courtroom. "The judge is ready for you now."

Jenna turned to them. "Remember, this is only a preliminary hearing. She's going to give her version, we'll give ours. This is not a trial. Yet."

The word hung ominously among them as Jenna turned on her heel and they followed her inside.

After what seemed an inordinate amount of time dealing with administrative details, the judge called the group to order.

Liza's lawyer stood up first. Cole noticed Jenna's back went ramrod straight. "Your honor, my client contests she should be awarded equal sharing of the lottery proceeds. She contributed to the lottery group longer than two of the current members."

Jenna stood. "Objection. Those members were current in their contributions to the kitty. The plaintiff was not." She returned to her seat.

"Her funds were still in the group's kitty for some time even after she left. Which, I'd like to stress to the court, the group did use to pay for their tickets."

Jenna returned to her feet, her attention on Liza's lawyer. "Ms. Skinner's contribution to the group's kitty did eventually run out, and she has not paid her way since then." Their lawyer remained standing this time.

Liza's lawyer angled toward Jenna. "We can cite examples where previously the others covered for someone who forgot to ante up. And there was no question as to whether they'd receive part of any prize if they won."

"Your client left no instructions prior to quitting her job at the television show and leaving. Nor any word of her intentions. For all the group knew, they'd never see her again, and therefore she'd forfeited her participation." Jenna faced the judge. "May I remind Your Honor that no written contract exists between the members as to the terms of the group. These details were left up to the existing group to decide."

"And may I remind both attorneys that this is a preliminary hearing. Not a battlefield." The judge stood, as well, her black robes flowing. "I need to see counsel in my chambers. Court is dismissed."

Eve turned to look at the rest of them, raising an eyebrow. "I'm not exactly sure what I saw, but that was something besides just arguing a case."

Cole couldn't agree more. This did not look good.

14

COLE PICKED UP JESSIE and they drove together to the cabin. It was Friday night and the first time they hadn't met somewhere, but she refused to denote any significance to the matter. Him driving was simply convenient. They'd chatted about frivolous stuff. The weather, the scenery outside, but what Jessie really wanted to talk about was the court case.

She'd read in the paper that Cole's group had met with the woman claiming she was due part of the money. No settlement had been reached as of yet, but surely now that a judge and lawyers were involved, something would be resolved quickly. Jessie could only imagine the kind of stress being in limbo caused.

She wanted to ask him if he was worried about losing all the money, since the millions would eventually go back to the state of Georgia if no clear claim was made. And what did he plan to do with the money if he did get it? Quit his job?

Cole seemed to be in a strange mood. Words had come easily between them at the restaurant, but now...

It was as if they were standing in an open doorway and they both had to make the choice whether to go through it or not. If they crossed the threshold, this fling would never be the same. They both had to know it.

Jessie twisted in her seat to ask when they'd arrive, just as Cole turned off the main road. As he steered along a country road the tree canopy grew thicker. The route became more winding. "We're almost there."

The houses she occasionally spotted were a fair distance apart, indicating large properties. "How much land do you have?"

"Roughly a hundred and twenty acres."

"Wow, that's a lot."

"We can explore it in the morning."

She cast him a sideways glance. Maybe that trip to the park late at night had given Cole the misimpression she was a camping kind of girl. Maybe she should try to distract him from those thoughts.

"I was thinking I'd explore your body." Ahh, a very pleasurable distraction.

A smile touched his lips as he pulled up in front of a rustic log cabin. She quickly scrambled out, anxious to stretch her legs, impatient to look around. Cole's place was like something out of a movie. A true log cabin that had a wraparound porch complete with a swing, welcomed her.

He hauled her suitcase out of the trunk. The air had grown cold, and she rubbed her hands up and down her arms for warmth.

"It won't take me long to get a fire going," he assured her as he headed up the gravel path.

Jessie followed him up the stone steps, loving the place on sight. Cole opened the front door and flipped on a light. His home was gorgeous inside. Open concept. A beautiful stone fireplace dominated one wall.

Tucked in a corner was a cozy kitchen. Cole shut the door behind her and she stared up to see exposed beams, and a stunning balcony that looked over the entire great room.

Family memorabilia graced the walls, and fluffy blankets and throw pillows invited lazy lounging with a book. This cabin was a home well loved. She'd fall asleep tonight with the smell of pine in the air.

"Cole, this is fantastic. I was thinking it would be rustic. We'd have to rough it."

Jessie jumped at the sound of their bags hitting the hardwood floor. She turned to look at Cole. He strode toward her. Purpose and thirst in his gaze.

She took a step back, then another until she touched the wall behind her. He trailed a finger down her cheek, cupped her chin and drew her lips toward his.

It was a kiss filled with need. Their mouths fused and their tongues entwined. She could almost taste the arousal on his lips. She leaned into him, giving as good as she got.

The slam of the heavy front door broke them

apart. The wind must have caught it. He leaned his forehead against hers, dragging in gulps of air.

"I wanted to do that the entire drive here."

She smiled, understanding the reason behind the strange mood in the car.

"I'll give you a tour after I get a fire going. There are two bedrooms upstairs, and a master downstairs."

He placed a light, quick kiss on her lips, then braced himself away from her. He walked toward the fireplace, his steps echoing throughout the cabin. She watched as the muscles of his arms bulged as he tossed a few logs onto the grate. Then he knelt and lit the kindling, taking care to get a strong flame going.

But Jessie didn't want a tour. She wanted those strong arms around her. They hadn't seen each other all week, and she was hungry now to feel the strength of him. The heat of him. To drag into her lungs that minty, citrusy smell of him.

All she wanted to do was toss one of those blankets in front of the fire and make love to Cole. She walked to him with purposeful steps. He straightened as she approached, his eyes growing darker. Oh, yeah, he knew what she intended.

"I don't want a tour."

"What do you want?"

Jessie reached up, wrapped her arms around his neck. "I want you." She gently tugged his head down. But that was the only thing gentle. Her kiss was urgent. And Cole met her need with a groan.

Then he pulled away. "I'm not going to let you drive me crazy. Not this time. This time it's going to be slow."

His thumb caressed her lower lip. "I love your mouth. I think about how damn good it feels nonstop."

Jessie leaned forward, ready to show him how good she could make him feel with her mouth.

"Not yet," he said without even a hint of teasing. Then she realized this wasn't a game for Cole. Tonight was about serious lovemaking.

He reached for her hand, gave it a gentle squeeze, and then drew her fingers to his lips. He lightly kissed each fingertip, then licked her palm.

She sucked in a breath, the sensation of his tongue there surprisingly erotic.

His mouth moved along, stroking the sensitive skin at her wrist, kissing the delicate, responsive area of her inner elbow. How flutters of excitement quaked and vibrated from such a simple caress she'd never know.

She also didn't care. Just wanted it to go on and on.

Cole's hand stroked up her arms. His fingers curled around her shoulders. With a sudden tug, he hauled her up against the hardness of his body.

"Your soft breasts against my chest...I couldn't think of anything else." His words became a moan and the rumble made her knees shaky. Cole's lips followed a lazy path along her neck and across her collarbone. Goose bumps tickled at her skin.

She ached to feel his hands on her breasts. The warmth of his breath, the moist torture of his tongue teasing her nipple.

He didn't make her wait. Her eyes closed at the first light brushing of his fingers.

Cole abruptly dropped his hands. "Open your eyes, Jessie. I want to see what you're feeling through your eyes."

She slowly lifted her lids and met the rich brown of his gaze. A smile tugged for the briefest of moments at his lower lip.

Then he cupped her from below. Lifted and molded her breasts with his hands, agonizingly staying away from her nipples.

He traced a circle pattern slowly around her. "This is what I'm going to do with my mouth. Over and over, moving closer and closer to your nipple. But I won't touch you there."

Her eyes narrowed.

"Not until you ask," he said, his voice seductive and filled with a kind of sexy confidence that said he knew she'd ask. Hell, she'd probably beg.

Her nipple tightened in anticipation, poking her shirt.

A cool blast of air hit her overheated skin as he slowly unbuttoned her blouse and guided it off her shoulders. His fingers lightly brushed her skin, creating a tight knot of sexual tension in her belly. He reached for the clasp of her bra. *Yes.* The scrap of material fell to the floor and that direct gaze he'd kept focused solely on her eyes dropped.

"Jessie, you're so beautiful," he said, his breath harsh.

He made her feel beautiful.

His gaze met hers again. "Now, on to the task at hand. You can close your eyes on this one," he said with a wink.

He lowered his head, his lips finding the stretch of skin where her breasts began to rise. He kissed slow circles against her skin, building her anticipation. Moving nearer and near toward her center. When he reached the darker hue of her areola he traced the outline with his tongue, circling closer and closer again but stopping before he reached his goal.

Her goal. She held her breath. Her muscles tensed. Every nerve ending tightened in sensual expectation. The delay of his mouth where she really wanted it was driving her crazy. She ached to feel his lips.

"Tell me what you want," he said against her sensitized skin. Her nipple puckered tighter.

"Take me into your mouth."

She shivered when his lips covered her nipple. But she moaned when he sucked it into his mouth.

Jessie sank her fingers into his scalp, wanting to draw him nearer. Cole shifted, giving the same, tormenting attention to her other breast as he'd given the first.

Her hands grew restless, gliding down the back of his neck. His shoulders. She twined her fingers into the soft material of his shirt. Frustration settled in her muscles. She didn't want to have this happen to her. She wanted to be a participant.

Now it was her turn to unbutton. Jessie pulled away from Cole's mouth, and their eyes met once more. Her eyes narrowed as he searched her gaze. She impatiently ripped off the top button on his shirt, their eye contact never breaking.

Jessie made herself slow down. To be seductive. She didn't want to show him just how desperate she was for him.

Jessie leaned forward and placed a kiss on his skin as she worked her way down with the buttons. His chest was magnificent, liberal with dark, curling hair and a few jagged scars. She kissed each mark. Cole was all lean muscles and flat stomach from his hard work. She had an image of lazily swinging on that swing outside, sipping iced tea while watching him chop wood.

She gave him a little of what he'd given her. Touching his skin with first her fingers, then her lips. His muscles flexed and tightened with her caress.

"I love it when you touch me," he said. The rawness of his voice making her slick and ready for him.

The pop and crackle of the fire mirrored her blood. "There," he said, angling his head toward the area before the fire. "I want to make love to you there."

He'd read her mind. "Yes." Her voice was little more than a sigh.

"Let me get a blanket."

Cole grabbed one of the flannel throws from off the couch and tossed it onto the floor, spreading it wide. He removed his jeans and shoes, and stretched naked on the blanket. An open invitation.

"Move in front of the fire, Jessie. I want to watch you take off your clothes with the glow of the flames on your skin."

She stepped in front of the massive stone fireplace, the warmth heating her naked back. She turned and faced him, loving the heat that entered his eyes when she thrust her breasts forward. She felt sexy and very, very wanted. Cole made her feel that way. Maybe she'd torture him with a slow striptease the way he'd tortured her earlier.

Jessie tugged at the button at the top of her jeans. Slowly rolled the zipper down, giving him a peek of the pink lacy panties. Yes, she'd chosen girlie pink. After hooking her fingers at the waistband, she rotated her hips to push the jeans lower. Then Jessie wiggled her legs as the material slid down her legs. She kicked them aside, standing before him in only her panties.

The sheerness of the pink material and the fire rendered those panties see-through. She turned, showing him her back and tugging the lace over her backside.

"You know what I want. I want to see all of you."

She squirmed out of her panties, then turned to face him. He closed his eyes and groaned at the fully naked sight of her.

"Don't close your eyes," she teased.

A smile tugged at his lips at her turning his own words around on him. Then he met her gaze. And the ache and longing she saw in those depths made her breath catch. She swallowed, all teasing vanished.

"Come here," he insisted, as he propped himself up on one arm. Jessie stepped forward and he reached for her. His hand stroked up her calf, sending hot thrills of tension between her legs. She wanted his touch everywhere. She wanted to touch him everywhere.

She sank to her knees beside him and reached for his cock. Although he'd pleasured her with his mouth, she hadn't reciprocated. That was about to change.

"I want to taste you," she told him. Her hair fell forward as she leaned over his body.

He groaned as he lay across the blanket. She wanted to tease him. Make him crazy, ready to beg. But tonight wasn't about the role-playing they'd done in bed before. Tonight was different, for some reason. Her heart was involved. Her mind participated. It wasn't just her body and her senses.

She licked her way up the side of his cock. Traced around the soft tip of him with her tongue. Then she took him fully into her mouth. He tensed and groaned below her. Jessie's whole body focused only on him.

She wanted to give and give to Cole. She continued to work him with her lips. Her tongue. Her mouth.

"Jessie, I want you now." He reached for her shoulders, pulling her up. "Put the condom on me."

She grabbed a packet by the hearth, ripping it open with her teeth. With fumbling fingers she stretched the latex down his shaft. Then she straddled him, ready to fill herself.

But Cole had other ideas. He enfolded her within his arms and gently rolled her onto her back.

"Look at me." His voice tight with need.

Her eyes drifted open. She could look into his gorgeous eyes forever.

"No games tonight," he said. "No playacting. Just you and me."

She nodded. "Yes. You and me."

He entered her then. Slowly slid inside her, and she gasped at the sheer pleasure of this unhurried and deliberate loving.

He drew himself away, only to thrust back inside.

She met him this time, drawing him deeper within her body. "Cole, that feels amazing."

"Just wait," he said, his voice strained and very, very sexy.

Their passion was hot and sweet. She wrapped her legs around his waist, locking her ankles behind his back. Wanting to get as close to him as she could. To never let this incredible intimacy end. They were sealed, their gazes locked, their hands together, their bodies joined. "Faster," she urged.

His movements slowed, and she almost groaned in frustration.

"No, you don't want faster. You want more." His voice an agonizing promise.

She wanted more and faster. And she wanted it now. She tried to take the rhythm away from him. His features grew harsh and strained. "Jessie, honey, when you do that, I can't stay slow."

"I don't want you to be slow."

His hips moved and he plunged within her, his thrusts quickening. He was hitting all the right places, and her inner tension built. She gripped him tighter, her orgasm within reach. His fingers slipped between then, and he stroked her clit.

She came then. Pleasure suffused every muscle. Every bone. His thrusts grew less deliberate. He stroked within her, then tensed. He groaned with his orgasm, the sound so raw and elemental that it almost triggered another orgasm within her.

He quieted, sucking in deep gulps of air. She did the same.

Then he spun onto his back, taking her with him. Cole tucked her to his side.

It was incredible. Unlike any of their sex in the past. Unlike any sex she'd had with anyone else.

"That was incredible," he said quietly, above her ear.

His words mimicked her thoughts. She'd clung to him. It was almost scary. They'd held hands as they made love. They kissed like people who cared about each other. Now she draped herself against his side. Incredible. Yes.

She nodded as her eyes drifted closed. She was warm from the fire. Sated from Cole. Her eyelids felt so very heavy....

How long she slept she didn't know, but she awoke with a start. She was covered by a blanket, but Cole was nowhere around. Jessie stood, awkwardly draping the blanket around her, sarong-style. She had an idea where she'd find him.

Jessie found him seated on the steps of the porch, deep in thought. She padded barefoot across the planked wood and sat beside him.

They didn't speak for several seconds. Just enjoying the night.

"The stars," she said, gazing up toward the sky. The first evening stars twinkled above them. Even though the sun hadn't set, she could already see more stars tonight than at home. Once full night fell, she'd probably be able to spot the Milky Way.

"You almost forget how many there are when you're always in the city. I didn't know how long you'd sleep, but I brought out two cups of coffee. Interested?"

She nodded, wrapping her fingers around the warm ceramic cup he handed her. He must not have been alone too long. The rich smell of the coffee blended with the piney freshness of the fall air.

"This is great. When did you start coming here?" she asked, knowing Cole's dad didn't have the kind of money for a place like this. If he had, it would have been sold a long time ago.

Cole let out a long breath. "Since I was seventeen. This is where my uncle took me, after your father called him. When I was discharged from the hospital, he picked me up and brought me here."

Almost no one had known where Cole had gone. Jessie's father would only say that he was okay, and that he would come back. But she'd been desperate to see him. To know for sure he was fine.

When Cole did return to school, he'd walked with a different kind of confidence. He'd been more serious, no longer such a rebel. He'd dropped out of every group. And he'd never asked for her help in Latin again.

Had that been her father's doing? Or was that Cole's decision?

His quick smile had vanished, too. She'd tried to meet up with him at his locker at school at least half a dozen times, but he'd always already left for class when she'd finally threaded her way through the between-class crowd. He'd never attended another school dance. It was only school, work and the small apartment above the garage. It was as if he'd completely ended his old life. And her with it.

She'd grown discouraged, realizing that whatever was between them had been one-sided. Then one afternoon in the school cafeteria, she felt a tingling sensation on the back of her neck. Looking over, her gaze collided with Cole's. His eyes were filled with such anguish and longing she gasped.

That yearning, which Jessie had spotted, gave her courage. She made the decision to get him alone after their graduation ceremony. She hadn't had much of a plan after that. She smiled sadly at her sixteen-year-old naïveté. She must have just hoped things would work out once she got him alone.

Of course, he'd skipped graduation, choosing instead to return to that unknown place he'd gone to in the summer.

The next time he'd returned to Thrasher, he had a fiancé, and she'd known it was never to be between them.

A light breeze ruffled her hair, and her nipples hardened against the blanket she'd brought from the floor. They may have missed their chance then, but she wasn't about to waste this opportunity now.

Jessie glanced in his direction. He scanned the trees, the bushes and late-blooming flowers. "This was my uncle's land. He left it to me." Cole was looking into the woods, but Jessie wasn't sure if he saw the trees or his memories.

"I was an ass. Angry at everyone and blaming everyone for what was happening at home. That first night, my uncle made me hike to a place by the river. You can't see it from here, but it's past that high ridge."

She looked where he pointed, trying to imagine the seventeen-year-old Cole out here.

"He gave me a canteen and a compass and left. Told me to find the cabin." Cole laughed, then took a swallow of coffee. "I walked around for hours, but finally saw the light of the fire through the windows. He'd made grilled cheese."

Cole turned toward her. "Best damn grilled cheese I'd ever had."

She nodded, knowing he didn't really need conversation right now. He just needed to talk.

"The next day we hiked up there again. This time he took my compass." Cole's voice was laced with a kind of humorous admiration as he spoke about his uncle.

"This must be some weird male thing, if you can appreciate it," she said.

He gave a low chuckle. "Maybe so." Then he shifted, facing her. His smile faded, the setting sun casting shadows across his strong features. "He made me face myself. Face being a man."

"You'd just gone through a horrible ordeal. And lived. I'm not sure leaving a kid out in the middle of nowhere is the way to go about helping. Your father—"

"Jessie, I was wallowing in it. Using that—my

father, my crappy childhood—as an excuse. Out there, with nothing but the stars and a half day's supply of water, I had to rely on myself. Learned that I *could* rely on myself. That I had the strength inside me to take on anything. The elements didn't care that I had a shit dad, or that I was poor. All I should focus on was how to survive. That's what I learned out here."

"That's why you return here."

Cole nodded. "Yes. There was only one thing I had to prove."

"What?"

"That the faith your father put in me wasn't wasted. He could have sent me to jail for stealing that car. But he smoothed it out. He made me pay for every cent of damage I did, but I worked extra on the weekends in the garage, and I had that money paid back in full by the time I graduated. I was damn lucky."

"How?" But she saw the truth in his words. Despite his rough beginnings, Cole lived his life like a man who thought he was lucky.

"I had people who believed in me. A lot of kids don't have that." His gaze lifted to the stars. "I wish there was a way I could help those kids, like someone helped me."

"That's what you want to do here, isn't it? With your lottery money, you want to set something up."

"Why don't I show you what I want to do?" He reached for her hand, pointing toward the ridge. "Slip into your shoes, and let's go."

Jessie quickly entered the cabin and donned her clothing. When she returned, Cole was waiting for her, carrying a flashlight. She lifted an eyebrow. "Did you have a flashlight when you were learning how to survive?" she teased.

He chuckled. "No, but I'm not seventeen anymore, and I have a hot, sexy woman with me, so I don't really need to stumble around in the dark."

She scanned the area, thinking about the lottery and what he could do with the money. "From what I read in the paper, you each chose your own number. What was yours?"

"46."

"Is that a special number?"

Cole shook his head. "No, I just read most people would choose their birth date or the age of a child. I did some research and found 46 is one of the least chosen numbers. It would be less likely someone else would choose it, so if we did win, there'd be no other winning tickets."

He reached for her hand again, and they walked toward the ridge. "I see rope courses over there. Camping and survival training past the river. Maybe a shop where kids can learn to fix cars. Some kind of skill training. And at the cabin, I see raising my girls. Together as a family again."

He spoke with a kind of hesitancy. As if putting voice to his dreams would jeopardize his plans. She knew why he was cautious. Understood his need to keep his dreams grounded. "But that won't happen if you don't get the money."

He squeezed her hand. "No. Even if Liza does relinquish her claim, there's always Amber."

The terrain grew more steep, and Jessie was glad she'd brought her boots.

"Amber would come after a piece of your winnings?"

He nodded. "Big-time."

"Tell me about her."

They'd finally crested the ridge, the river down below. She watched the current, followed the progress of a branch on the water.

Finally, Cole spoke. "Amber was everything I thought I was supposed to want. I think I fell in love with her the first time I saw her. She was funny, and always up for an adventure. She made me forget about the past. Forget about my mistakes and just live."

It should have hurt to hear him talk about his ex-wife like this. How he'd loved another woman. But for some reason it helped.

Jessie understood him better.

Cole hadn't been rejecting her all those years ago. He'd just been looking for something different. Something she couldn't provide for him.

If he hadn't found Amber, he wouldn't be the man he was today. The man she lo—

Oh, hell.

She loved him.

Jessie had a sick feeling in her stomach.

An hour ago she'd made love like a woman in love. She'd even thought of it as lovemaking.

She was talking to a man about his dreams and aspirations like a woman in love. She broke out in a cold sweat.

Now she was encouraging a man to speak about the mistakes he'd made…like a woman in love would do.

"She understood me. My past. She'd been in some trouble, too. Shoplifting, that kind of thing. Getting married seemed like the reasonable, mature thing to do. We both had something to prove. The twins came along quickly. But truly settling down wasn't what Amber wanted."

The wind picked up, ruffling Cole's hair. Jessie should have grabbed a jacket.

He sighed. "We came to an agreement. She left the twins with me, and I helped her out of a jam."

A jam. Jessie bet that small word contained a multitude of problems Amber had caused for herself. She shivered, and Cole wrapped his arm around her.

"So far she's kept her side of the bargain. She's stayed away. But if that money comes through… she'll be back, and I'll have to be prepared."

He turned and started toward the cabin. They strolled in silence, listening to the breeze rustling the tree limbs, and the crickets singing their sad, night song.

Cole had shared himself with Jessie tonight. She doubted many people knew the real details of his life, and she felt a little shaken that he'd chosen to be so candid. Emotions. Sharing. *So* not in the rules of a fling.

THE REST OF THEIR WEEKEND passed in a pleasurable haze of lovemaking, the days spent exploring the woods and the nights lazing in front of the fire. But by late Sunday afternoon they were back on the highway to Atlanta.

Cole pulled up in front of her house, and suddenly Jessie felt at a true loss as to what to do. She'd come to a lot of realizations over the weekend, primarily that she loved the man sitting beside her.

But now the holiday was over, and she needed to do some thinking without the love haze Cole created.

"What do you want to do tomorrow night?" Cole asked as he carried her luggage inside.

"Tomorrow? Did we make plans for tomorrow night?"

"No."

Were they actually at the stage where they assumed they'd do whatever together just because they were…together?

Jessie leaned against the door frame. "Let's just play it by ear."

His eyes narrowed. "What do you mean?"

"I mean, this is just a fl—"

"Do not say *fling*," he interrupted. His face hardened. "I don't ever want to hear that word again as long as I live."

"Then what do you think it is?"

"A relationship. Although I hate *that* word, too." He looked away from her, his body a study in frustration. Then he turned and their eyes met. "We're two people who are together."

Her heartbeat quickened, and she felt a sick sensation in her stomach. "No. This is just fun. No plans."

"Jessie, I want to ask 'What are we doing tonight?' instead of wondering if I'll see you or not. I *want* plans. I want to fall asleep with you. Wake up with you. Although the games are great, I want to make love with you, too."

She didn't want this. Didn't want to need those things. She'd wanted them with Keith, and look where it had gotten her. "Why can't we keep it fun?"

Cole reached out and cupped her face, his thumb caressing her bottom lip. A shock of sweet desire pounded in her blood.

"Because I love you, Jessie. I've fallen in love with you."

Jessie now realized her mistake in trusting in the myth of the bad boy. A boy used that persona to mask his longings, what he ached for. But Cole wasn't hiding. He wanted her.

She stepped away from him, not able to handle his touch. "I don't want to be in love, Cole. I don't want you to love me. It's too hard. Hurts too much when it doesn't work out."

"Yeah, I was married to a woman who kicked my heart around for sport. But I'm still willing to give it a shot."

"This, what we have right now, is what I'm willing to try."

He looked shocked for a moment. Cole took a step away from her as if she'd hit him. "Then it has to end here."

"Why?"

She saw the sadness in his eyes. "Because I'll always want more from you, Jessie."

She forced herself to act casual, not wanting to appear cruel or cold. But she needed to make Cole understand. "I'm sorry. This is all I have to give."

"Then I guess that's all you have to say."

15

JESSIE HUELL WAS IN A relationship.

Dammit.

It had only taken her two days to realize it. Of course, she'd pretty much blown that new relationship apart on Sunday evening, but she'd still been in one for at least a while.

How had this happened?

She'd got caught up in the rules of the fling, and forgot to remind herself about the dangers of the man.

Cole Crawford loved her, and that was a devastating reality.

She loved *him*. Felt torn inside without him. How had he done it? How had he sneaked under every defense she had?

And with that love, all the baggage, all the insecurity that came with it would surely follow. Right?

It would be only a matter of time before she found herself knocking on his apartment door. Making up some cutesy excuse, like demanding he stop holding her fedora hat like a common criminal. Pathetic, really, but right now she'd grab at any chance to be alone with him and hear him say he loved her again.

Jessie Huell wanted to stay in that relationship.

She had tried to bury herself in work. Two intense days with the Brocks had, sadly, yielded nothing. They hadn't recognized the man in her photo. She'd tried a little reverse surveillance, following them to see if maybe their blackmailer would be following them still. Their plan was to find him and then call the police.

He'd given them a deadline of this weekend to come up with a staggering amount of money or he'd go to the media with his pictures. The Brocks' desperation to find out his identity before their secret was spilled had become a palpable thing. The situation seemed to add five years to both of them. Mayor Brock, a woman Jessie admired, had grown quiet and cautious because her secrets were about to be made public.

And secrets made her think of Cole.

Cole was still a man with many secrets. Jessie had sensed them around him. But what was there left to tell? What was he trying to protect? Who?

What's the one thing she stressed to women before they entered a relationship? Find out all the dirt, because there was always dirt. She was so far behind the curve here with Cole. She had to find out what she was dealing with. She'd grown a little panicky herself.

Where did he go at night?

What did he do?

Maybe it was time to put her investigative skills to work.

Finally. Relief drove away some of her anxiety. Finally she had a plan. She didn't have to meet the Brocks until tomorrow, and her other cases wouldn't become top priority until the end of the week.

She could spend the rest of her day playing catch-up on Cole. If she had to be in love, she'd at least arm herself, knowing all there was to know about the man.

Jessie drove to his apartment, only to be surprised when she spotted him walking down the staircase toward his car.

Figures.

What was even more surprising was the movement of a head ducking below the seat in a car several rows away from his.

Now this was an interesting development. Jessie tapped on her steering wheel as she waited for the light to change. A sense of déjà vu assailed her. Someone else was spying on Cole, the same way someone unknown had spied on the Brocks. This time Jessie wouldn't push it aside. This time she'd find out why.

Cole drove out of the parking lot and headed for the highway. A brown compact pulled out behind him. Keeping to his exact path.

Jessie smiled. The chase was on.

She flipped on her radio and relaxed in her seat.

This was something she was comfortable with. She'd hoped that maybe the brown car was a coincidence. That maybe after a few turns, the vehicle would head in another direction.

No such luck.

Five minutes into the trip, Jessie grew thankful she wouldn't have to worry about losing him in the traffic. Based on Cole's direction, he was heading for the cabin. How could that be? It didn't make sense. She eased back from the brown car. No reason to tip him or her off.

The car following Cole dropped back, too, whoever it was obviously familiar with his route.

Not a good sign.

As they progressed, both Jessie and the brown car fell farther and farther behind. As the traffic thinned, and Cole turned off the highway, their presence would be even more noticeable.

Jessie allowed herself to get a full ten minutes behind Cole. Surely that would give him enough time to reach the cabin. Luckily, after last weekend, she was familiar with the lay of the land. She could conceal her car at the base of the drive and hike up to the house to get a better vantage point.

Jessie followed that plan, until the log cabin slowly came into view. Cole was walking across the clearing as she approached, and she ducked behind some bushes. She took a few deep, calming breaths. No sense in alerting him to her presence. Her nerves grew cool. Her muscles tensed in quiet expectation. This was her element. What she was good at. She had advantages here, in that she already knew the layout of Cole's cabin. Although, she'd been a little too busy jumping that man's body to do any really decent surveillance. She hadn't noted the best outside hiding spaces.

Apparently, she'd been too busy to note a lot of things, because what she was seeing right now was Cole with a shovel. Digging.

What the—

Was he burying something? Or retrieving?

So much for he only came out here on weekends. This was definitely suspicious. *Here* was the dirt she'd expected all along. A man didn't reach Cole's age without a lot of dirt. Her breath came out in a sad sigh. She'd been hoping…

Jessie shifted silently, preparing to crouch there, hidden, for as long as she needed to.

What she wasn't prepared for was the woman crowding behind another bush.

Just how many women was Cole stringing along right now?

This was why Jessie didn't want a relationship. Why she didn't want to fall in love. She didn't want to feel angry. Jealous. Hurt.

Cole stopped his digging, bent and pulled from the ground a black sack of some kind.

That's when the woman behind the bush stood up,

her red hair flowing. Jessie caught a quick look at her face. Amber. Cole's ex-wife. She'd seen her once or twice in the early days of their relationship. Jessie had put an end to her weekend visits to see her parents for almost a semester so she wouldn't accidentally run into the happy pair.

By Thanksgiving of her freshman year in college, Jessie realized she was being ridiculous. She reminded herself that she liked Cole enough to be happy for him and she could greet them both on the street with a smile. By her sophomore year, he'd stopped coming to Thrasher, and she was both sad and relieved.

It was supposed to be over. He'd assured Jessie it was. She took a deep, calming breath. She'd believed him.

"Cole, let me have them," Amber yelled.

Well, that was one way the woman could use the element of surprise. Had Jessie wanted that sack, she'd have grabbed for it before he was truly alerted to her presence.

Cole tucked the sack into the back of his jeans, his expression resigned. He'd been expecting her. Maybe that's why he'd been trying to move them. To take them to another, more secure hiding place?

"I need them, Cole."

"These are my insurance policy, Amber. We had a deal, remember? I didn't turn these over to the police and you stayed away from me and the girls."

Amber began to softly cry, her beautiful face turning red. "I'm scared, Cole. I really messed up this time. Harton, he knows it's me who stole the coins. He's going to send someone after me. One of his associates is going to kill me."

Cole shook his head. Even from Jessie's hiding spot, she could tell his every muscle was tight with frustration. "The people you're calling associates. Amber, would you listen to yourself? You need to get out of this. Get out of this lifestyle. Turn yourself in. A judge would take that into consideration in sentencing. You could finish college in prison. Do something other than this."

"Cole, would you can it with all the 'be a better person' crap? It's not like I didn't get enough of that in our marriage. You used to be a lot more fun."

How cold could this woman be? She hadn't even asked Cole about her children.

Cole's expression turned grim. "Marriage to you has a way of killing all the fun."

Amber's tears stopped abruptly and her body language softened. She trailed her fingers down his arm. That bitch. Was she trying to seduce him now?

"I know, and I'm sorry. Let me make it up to you. We can go abroad. Sell the coins. We could live like kings for years."

He shrugged. "Until what? Until the money ran out or until Harton's people found us? Leave the girls for Annie and George to raise?"

"I don't know." Amber's voice lost its seductive

edge. Now she just sounded scared and tired. "I haven't planned that far."

Cole shook his head. "No, I'm going to turn these over to the police myself. That's what I should have done in the first place instead of making that bargain with you. Being an accessory to a crime doesn't sit well."

"Yeah, like Harton is a model citizen. Hardly a crime. Who knows what he did to get them. The police would probably give me a medal for stealing from him."

"Not a convincing argument." He kicked at a clot of dirt by his boot. "I have to give them back."

Amber's hands gripped Cole's arm. "You can't," she said, her tone desperate. "Then I'll have nothing. Please give me the coins, Cole. You'll never see me again. I *have* to disappear."

That would do it. Jessie knew without a doubt now that Cole would give her those coins.

He yanked the sack from his back pocket. Amber sucked in a breath. "You know you can never return to the United States. If you take these and sell them, staying away is your only chance."

Amber nodded. "I know."

He held the sack out, but did not let her tug it from his hand. "There's always the option of turning yourself in."

Cole's ex-wife shrugged. "Would I look good in orange?"

His shoulders sagged in disappointment. Jessie understood now his attraction to Amber. He'd wanted to save her. Save her like his uncle had saved him.

Only Amber didn't want to be saved.

She pulled the sack from his hand, closing her eyes for a moment. "Thank you, Cole. Thank you."

Who could doubt the fear and relief in her voice?

"Take care of yourself," he said.

She looked as if she wanted to kiss him, but instead gave him a sad smile and turned away. She stopped a few paces later and glanced back at him. "You can always come with me. We could have a lot of fun."

"No. I belong here." His voice was final.

"You with someone?" she asked.

She saw him shake his head, then reach for the shovel. With frustrated swipes, he refilled the hole.

So that was Cole's dirt. Literally and figuratively.

Jessie watched him a few more minutes before he disappeared inside the cabin.

AFTER A SLEEPLESS NIGHT during which she was tempted to call Cole about a hundred times, Jessie finally just rolled out of bed. A little prework for a case never hurt anyone. Besides, she had a long conversation with the Brocks ahead of her.

Three hours later they were gathered in the seating area in her inner office.

"Whoever this guy is, he's good. He's not followed you since, and he's avoided every conceivable trap. My advice now is to go to the police so they can develop a sting when you're ready to drop the money."

"The media. There's no way they won't find out," the mayor said, staring into her coffee cup.

Tom Brock had been pacing the length of Jessie's office, but now sank into the chair beside his wife, rubbing the back of his neck.

"That's it then," the mayor continued. "We'll go to the police. What's more, if we have to, we'll make a full disclosure to the media. Call a press conference. If my private life has to be made public, at least it will be done on my terms."

There it was again. That strength Jessie had so admired in her.

The woman's shoulders sagged. "I can still do good in Knightsville as mayor."

"You can do good in other ways," her husband said.

Jessie heard the pain in his voice. The agony he felt for his wife probably having to leave a job he knew she loved.

Then Jessie watched as this powerful woman, who had such big responsibilities, leaned against her husband's side and drew comfort.

Jessie felt a pang in her own heart.

Amy Brock stretched and set her coffee cup on the end table. The woman looked relieved. The stress and anxiety were vanishing from her face. "You know, I thought it would be the end of the world if I lost this election. I would have done anything to avoid it. It was the absolute worst thing I could imagine. But losing you, Tom—that would be the worst thing that could happen. We'll get through this together."

He squeezed her hand. "Come on, I'll take you home."

The Brocks held hands as they exited Jessie's office. They were in love. They really were. So they had a thing for unusual foreplay. Who cared? It could be a lot worse.

A strong ache ripped through Jessie. She reveled in it, in her ability to feel. She didn't want a fling. She didn't want to be intimidated by the word *relationship*. She wanted what she'd just witnessed. Two people sharing their lives together. She liked how Cole had described it.

To take strength. To give strength. Cole's love, and her love for him, didn't make her weak. It actually made her stronger.

Cole wasn't Keith. He'd shown her time and time again he could be trusted. How he kept the secret about the mayor. The way he loved his daughters. Even the way he protected his ex-wife.

Suddenly, Jessie was impatient to talk to him. She burned to be with him. She didn't want to wait until this afternoon when the show would be over.

She locked up her office and headed to the TV station, running through a dozen scenarios in her mind. This had to be the mother of all grovels. He'd told her he loved her, and she'd practically thrown it in his face. That had to hurt.

She had major amends to make.

It would be worth it to see Cole's smile, though. To be held in his arms. To know he still loved her.

Jessie rushed through the glass doors of the station, forgetting about security. She'd wanted to surprise him. Not give him the chance to close himself off to her for the rest of their lives.

But this was reality. She'd have to sit and wait for him. It was probably only for a few minutes since the receptionist had announced her, but it felt like an hour before he arrived.

He turned the corner. Cole looked so good. Tired, but good.

She smiled at him. Couldn't help it. Just gave him the biggest I-love-you-so-much-I-don't-care-who-sees-it smile.

He seemed shocked. Then he glanced toward the receptionist. "I'm going to take her back with me." He leaned down and signed what she spotted was a guest register.

They walked side by side down the hallway. Was it just a few weeks ago they'd done the exact same thing? Then, she'd been nervous because she was about to make an idiot of herself on live TV. Now, she was nervous because if she didn't do this right, she'd lose him forever.

He shut the door behind her. Her normal self would do a quick assessment of his office. Try to glean clues about the man based on his surroundings. But she didn't need to do that. Jessie knew all she needed to know about Cole Crawford.

He leaned against the closed door. His expression was neutral, but his eyes burned with curiosity.

"I want to be with you." Okay, not one of the scenarios she'd worked up in her mind on the drive over here. Blurting that out like that. But she was committed now. She might as well go for it.

She would run to him if she thought it'd make a difference. "Cole, I've been hurt bad. I had an ex who cheated on me, and there's the business—where I see a lot of the worst side of love. I'm a cynic. Until you, I didn't believe love could really exist between a man and a woman."

"Until me?"

She nodded, reaching up and placing her hands on his shoulders. Feeling the heat of his body. "We can call this whatever we want. A relationship. Just being together. A few days ago you asked me to give you more and I said I couldn't. I was wrong. I can give you everything. I love you, Cole."

His eyes closed at her words. She saw him swallow, and a tiny thrill shivered down her body. She did this to him. Made him happy.

His lips found hers in a gentle kiss. A promise.

"I have so much to tell you. You feel like taking a drive later?" he asked.

"Tonight?" She had visions of hot sex scheduled in her mind. Not a drive.

Cole nodded. "I have two people I want you to meet."

Jessie caught the heartfelt look in his eyes.

His daughters. Cole wanted to take her to meet his little girls. This was his big step. He didn't have to say another word. He saw a future with her in it. Sharing his life. Sharing his family.

Was this what she wanted? It would be tough. Stepmothers were never portrayed well in movies. But then…she did like glitter.

With a smile, Jessie slipped her hand into his. He gave her a firm squeeze, their fingers twining. "I'd like that."

* * * * *

Don't miss the final installment of
MILLION DOLLAR SECRETS
Will the gang win their millions?
Will Liza triumph?
Find out in
WHAT SHE REALLY WANTS FOR CHRISTMAS
available next month from Harlequin Blaze.
Turn the page for a sneak peek....

1

RUMOR HAS IT THAT Atlanta's own Just Between Us, *the three-year-old, sex-themed, hot-topic afternoon television show hosted by Eve Best, is soon going into national syndication. Geared toward women's perspectives and concerns, the local show has garnered a widely growing audience, and advertisers have taken notice. While the program has taken on contemporary, cutting-edge topics, Ms. Best's own energy and spontaneity have captured the attention of teens and mothers alike.*

Recently, however, the local show has drawn a maelstrom of publicity not so flattering. Most of you already know about the state lottery win, shared by six employees of the show, including Ms. Best. But what this reporter has just learned is that despite attempts to keep the unpleasantness quiet, a lawsuit filed by a former segment producer, Liza Skinner, has halted the disbursement of the winnings.

According to my source, Ms. Skinner was an original member of the lottery pool before leaving the show nearly a year ago. There is some confusion as to whether she still had money in the pot, but the number 13, which she'd chosen, was among the six winning numbers, and apparently she seems to think she deserves a share.

Liza quit reading the article and threw the copy of last week's *Atlanta Daily News* onto the passenger seat of her compact car. When she got home, she was throwing the tattered paper away. No use continuing to torture herself. The wheels were already in motion. Soon, it would be all over. She hoped.

She pushed a shaky hand through her tangled hair and tried to get comfortable, not easy with her long legs. She had no business being here. Her attorney had told her to stay away from the *Just Between Us* studio. At least, until her lawsuit was settled. Although then there'd be no reason to be here, in the parking lot, waiting, like a smitten schoolgirl, for a glimpse of Eve and Jane. No matter which way the suit went, her friends would never speak to her again.

She didn't blame them. All she'd done in the past year was cause them pain. Hadn't they warned her about Rick? From the start, they'd known he'd be trouble. They'd been her best friends since the sixth grade, closer to her than anyone in the whole world. Why hadn't she listened to them?

Liza let her head fall back against the worn cloth upholstery and forced herself to breathe. He'd been just her type, wild and sexy and a little dangerous, and she'd thought he was the one. He turned out to be more dangerous than she'd ever imagined.

Movement caught her eye and she turned her head just in time to see a woman step outside, the sunlight glimmering off her pale blond hair. She looked like Nicole, the *Just Between Us* segment producer who'd replaced Liza. The woman who was going to get Liza's share of the lottery money. Unless the lawsuit was successful.

God, why didn't they just pay up? It wasn't as if each of them wasn't going to still be filthy rich after coughing up her share. She closed her eyes, blocking out the image of the woman walking toward a red convertible. A reminder of how much Liza had lost. Just another month and it would all be over.

Of course, if she had the guts, she could go to Eve and Jane now. Confess everything. The idea took hold, her breathing quickening. Slowly, she opened her eyes. Could it be that simple? After nearly a year of selling her soul? Ha. Sure, confessing would ease her conscience, but that wouldn't solve anything. Eve would still be vulnerable to public humiliation. And it would still be Liza's fault.

She hung her head and stared at her painful cuticles. Nowadays she couldn't even afford a manicure. The small inheritance she'd received after her father's death last year was nearly gone, and there was rent to pay, attorney's fees and a myriad of other things. But what she resented the most was the money Rick spent on cigarettes, booze and drugs. Money she could've used to buy a better car, live in a better neighborhood.

Maybe when this was over she'd be able to find a decent job. Never one like she'd had with *Just Between Us*. That had been a dream job. The once-in-a-lifetime kind. She knew, because she'd been a part of it from the beginning. Those crazy, fifteen-hour days when none of them knew what they were doing, but they pushed forward, tackling any task they were given, their passion making up for what they'd lacked in experience.

Their hard work had paid off. The show was a huge success. This should have been the best time in Liza's life. But she was no longer a part of her friends' lives or a part of the show. All because of her stupidity. Even if Eve and Jane eventually forgave her, she seriously doubted she could forgive herself.

Eve walked out of the redbrick building, and Liza bit down on her lower lip. The radiance in her friend's face made Liza's stomach knot. Behind her was the reason for Eve's glow. Tall, good-looking, with dark hair, the man put a familiar hand at the small of Eve's back.

Liza had heard Eve had found someone. Mitch Hayes, the guy who once represented the television network that first tried to sign on *Just Between Us*. She looked happy. Happier than Liza had ever seen her.

Damn. No way was Liza getting her friends involved now. She'd push for the settlement, pay off Rick and then she'd disappear. Start a new life where no one knew her. Where she wouldn't be considered scum of the earth.

And never see her friends again.

Liza squeezed her eyes shut, willing the threatening tears away. At least Eve would be spared any humiliation. A tear escaped, and Liza swiped at it angrily. Crying wouldn't solve a damn thing. Never had. Never would. She scrubbed at her eyes, disgusted at the display of weakness.

And then she heard something. The sound of knocking. At the car window.

Opening her eyes, she swung her face toward the sound. A man with short dark hair and concerned brown eyes stared back at her. It took a moment to recognize him…the doctor who consulted for the medical drama shot in the studio next to *Just Between Us*. Dr. Evan something. He'd asked her to lunch once. She'd blown him off. Sedate and conservative. Definitely not her type.

She took another furtive swipe at her eyes, annoyed that he might have seen her crying. When he motioned for her to let down her window, she was tempted to ignore him. But that was bound to make matters worse, and the last thing she needed was to create a scene in front of the station.

Lucky she could afford a car at all, she didn't have the luxury of automatic windows and manually rolled hers down. He ducked his head, gripping the top of the door, and smiled. She didn't.

"Liza, hi." He paused. "Remember me?"

She deliberately frowned and gave a small shake of her head. If the slight embarrassed him, maybe he'd leave her alone.

"Evan Gann." He inclined his head toward the building. "From the studio next to *Just Between Us*."

"Oh, right. You're the consultant."

He nodded, his eyes probing. "I haven't seen you for a while."

"I'm persona non grata around here. Surely, you've heard."

"Ah, the lawsuit." His eyebrows drew together. "I don't know the details—"

"You wanted something."

His mouth curved in an annoyingly tolerant smile. "I was surprised to see you. Look, you want to have a drink sometime?"

"Why?"

He chuckled. "Because you're attractive and I like you?"

It took Liza a moment to collect herself. Was this guy nuts? He'd probably be banned from the station just for talking to her. She frowned. Except he really wasn't nuts. He was this straightlaced, normal kind of guy. "I've got too much going on right now." She reached for the knob to roll up the window, and when he didn't move, she said, "Do you mind?"

"Why don't you take my number for when you have some time? I'll buy you dinner."

"Look, Evan, you're a nice guy but—"

"Thought you didn't remember me?" His slow, teasing grin did something to the inside of her chest.

She almost smiled. "See you around," she said, and this time when she attempted to roll up the window, he let go and stepped away. She started the engine, reversed out of the parking spot and drove off without looking back.

EVAN REACHED INTO his pocket for his car keys and used the remote to unlock the doors. His silver Camry was parked right next to the spot Liza had vacated. That was the only reason he'd noticed her, sitting behind the wheel of the small white compact, crying. Wisely, he hadn't mentioned that. From what he knew of her, she wasn't the type of woman who indulged herself with tears. In fact, from what he'd heard around the station, she'd been more prone to express her anger or pain with a few choice words.

Still, the lawsuit she'd launched didn't add up. Until a year ago, Liza, Eve and Jane had been inseparable. He'd admired their loyalty and friendship. The show was really taking off, thanks to Eve Best's charismatic personality and Liza's creative genius. And then suddenly, Liza had disappeared. No one seemed to know why she'd left or where she went, although he suspected Eve and Jane knew more than they'd admitted. It was their business, but that didn't stop him from being curious.

Mostly because he'd liked Liza from the first time he'd met her. He'd been on his way to the set of the medical drama when he'd bumped into her. Literally. She'd been talking to someone over her shoulder and hadn't seen him come around the corner. Abruptly, she'd turned and plowed right into him. Unfortunately for him, she'd been holding a cup of coffee.

He smiled when he thought about how she'd tried to right the wrong, using her napkin to blot his suit, regardless of where the coffee had landed. When she'd finally realized that pressing the napkin to his crotch might not have been the wisest move, she'd looked him in the eye, apologized and asked to be given the cleaning bill.

No nervous twittering or inane remarks. She wasn't like so many of the women he met, either on the set or at dinner parties hosted by his well-intentioned friends determined to find him a wife. Liza was straightforward, to the point, and he liked that. Normally, he preferred blondes, which made his attraction to her all the more curious, since she was tall, with long, unruly brown hair.

Not that it mattered. He'd asked Liza out to lunch once, and in her no-nonsense fashion, she'd turned him down flat. No excuses, no little white lies to let him off easy. Just a frank refusal that told him not to ask again. After that there was the occasional exchange of greetings when they passed each other in the lobby or parking lot.

Realizing he was still staring after her long-gone car, he opened the door of his Camry and slid behind the wheel. Eve had walked out of the building ahead of him, but obviously she wasn't the reason Liza had been here. So why *was* she here? More importantly, why did he care? She'd just shot him down again.

It was so late by the time Liza got home that there wasn't a single parking spot left in the complex, and she had to park a block away from her apartment. Sighing, she cut the car's engine and then grabbed the bag of burgers she'd picked up from a drive-through. She really hated parking on the street. Especially in this crappy neighborhood. Hopefully, any thieves would go for the nice new black sedan parked in front of her.

Not that she loved her secondhand lemon of a car. But if something happened to it, she couldn't afford to buy another one. Rick had naturally insisted on buying a brand-new Harley-Davidson for himself. With her money. Amazing he hadn't cracked it up yet. Not that it would hurt her feelings if he did. In fact, in her more stressed out moments, she'd actually wished he would. He didn't have to die or anything, just end up in a coma for a good five years.

She slowed her steps, just thinking about how he lived in the apartment right next to hers, and that if he happened to look out of the window, he'd see her walk up the stairs. Inevitably, he'd come outside and grill her about where she'd been. His language would be foul and he wouldn't give a damn about who overheard. But if she was lucky, he'd be passed out and she wouldn't have to deal with him until tomorrow.

Sighing, she took the first few stairs, her gaze darting toward Rick's door, praying, hoping she'd have an evening of peace and quiet. So far, so good…

"Hey, Liza, what you got in the bag?"

The sound of her new neighbor's high-pitched voice made Liza cringe. She waved for Mary Ellen to keep it down, and then, with one eye on Rick's door, she hurried the rest of the way to the third floor.

Leaning over the railing, which was decorated with a string of large, colored Christmas lights, Mary Ellen waited, dutifully keeping her mouth shut until Liza joined her. "I think he's passed out," the younger woman said in that strange drawl of hers.

She claimed that she and her kid were from Mississippi, but Liza had her doubts. The apartment complex's residents weren't exactly members of mainstream society. At least once a week Liza heard a shot being fired nearby, or watched the police drag away an abusive husband or boyfriend. But the rent was cheap, and since she had to fork out money for both her place and Rick's, this was the best she could afford.

Rick had thought it was stupid to have separate apartments, mostly because he wanted complete control over her. But that was the one thing she wouldn't negotiate with him. She didn't care that she'd end up broke, but as threadbare as it was, her sanity wasn't something she was ready to lose. And she sure didn't need him in her face.

She reached the third-floor landing and furtively peeked into Rick's open window. Sure enough, he lay flat on his back on the tattered brown corduroy couch that they'd picked up at a thrift store. An empty vodka bottle sat on the end table, but she knew he'd consumed more than booze. Good. Maybe she could have a quiet meal with Mary Ellen and her daughter.

"Told ya." Mary Ellen inclined her dirty-blond head toward Rick's apartment, but her gaze stayed on the fast-food bag.

"Hungry?"

"Starving."

"I bought extra burgers for you and Freedom."

Mary Ellen broke into a wide grin that displayed a missing back tooth, which wasn't usually noticeable since she didn't smile much. "Oh, goody. I thought we were gonna have to eat macaroni and cheese again." She turned around, put two fingers into her mouth and let out an ear-piercing whistle.

Liza cringed. With dread, she took a step back and squinted into Rick's apartment. He was still out cold. However, Freedom heard her mom's whistle and came bounding up the stairs.

"Hi, Liza." The eight-year-old tomboy was covered with dirt. She pulled off her red ball cap, and dust flew everywhere. "Time for dinner?" she asked her mom, her hopeful blue eyes going to the bag.

"Liza bought us burgers."

"Yahoo. Fries, too?"

Liza unlocked her apartment door. "They would've gotten cold."

"The hamburgers are cold, too," Freedom stated, with perfect logic.

"That's true," Mary Ellen said, her slight frown accentuating the scar paralleling her lower lip.

Sighing, Liza led them inside and went straight to the microwave. Eating cold French fries wasn't the same thing, but Liza didn't want to get into it with them. She wanted them to eat and leave. In fact, she should've given them the food to take back to their own apartment, but she had a soft spot for Mary Ellen and her daughter.

As pitiful as Liza's place was, with its chipped paint and stained, olive-green carpet, the other two managed to live in a cheaper cramped studio apartment. Mary Ellen still ended up two months behind on the rent, since her welfare checks didn't quite cover all their expenses. With her pronounced limp, she'd had trouble finding a job that would support the two of them. Liza had never asked her about the bum leg, but she had a bad feeling about it.

She finished nuking the burgers, and Mary Ellen had already put napkins on the small table. It was only big enough for two, so Freedom sat on her mother's good knee. She quickly wolfed down her burger, and eyed a second one. Liza pushed it across to her, wishing she'd bought more than five sandwiches. When Mary Ellen finished hers, Liza offered her the last one.

"What about Rick?"

Amazing how just the mention of him could knot her stomach and make the hair on her neck stand up. "What about him?"

"Isn't he eating?"

"Don't know. Don't care."

Mary Ellen regarded her quizzically. "Why do you stay with him?"

"I'm not *with* him." Liza grabbed the used wrappers and crumpled them as she got to her feet. She'd seen the curious looks Mary Ellen had given her on the unfortunate occasions when Rick was drunk and he'd yelled from the door of his apartment as Liza was trying to slip quietly down the stairs. But she didn't intend to discuss her problems with Mary Ellen. Or anyone else.

"Why do you live next door to him then?" the other woman asked.

Liza disposed of the wrappers, using the time to compose herself. Anyone else and she would have told them it was none of their damn business. But having to look into Mary Ellen's perpetually sad eyes, Liza just couldn't do it.

"It's complicated," she said finally.

"That means you don't want to talk about it, huh?" the little girl mumbled, her mouth full.

"Freedom," Mary Ellen admonished her. "This is grown-up talk. You be quiet."

Liza hid a smile. Poor kid was going to grow up to be like her. Smart-mouthed and always in trouble.

"You went to college, didn't you?" Mary Ellen asked.

Liza slowly nodded, not liking the conversation.

"You're so pretty and smart, and I don't understand why you'd be living in a dump like this."

Right. Real smart. So smart that she'd put herself in a position to be blackmailed. "Look," Liza said in a tight voice, casting a brief glance at Freedom, who'd turned to licking her fingers instead of listening to the conversation, "I don't think you want to start a question-and-answer session."

Mary Ellen looked grimly down at her weather-roughened hands. "No," she said quietly, and then cleared her throat and rose from the table. "Freedom, come on. We need to be going. Thanks for dinner, Liza." Mary Ellen pulled her daughter along with her, keeping her face toward the door.

"See you later." Liza stayed in the small open kitchen and watched them go. She probably should've made nice. Mary Ellen hadn't meant anything by what she'd said. The woman seemed to have such a lonely life, she probably only wanted to talk.

But Liza just couldn't do it. Not today. Everything

had gone wrong. After being decisive all of her life, she'd become as stable as a palm tree in a hurricane. She should never have allowed the blackmail to get this far, but she'd panicked, and everything had spiraled out of control before she knew what had happened. Winning the lawsuit would save her ass, if she could only keep her act together.

She walked to the love seat and sank down, careful to avoid the bad spring in the center. God, was this headache ever going away? She leaned forward, rested her elbows on her knees and cradled her head in her hands. She needed a couple of aspirin. But that meant going out to get them. No way. She was staying right where she was to enjoy the peace and quiet while Rick was passed out.

Going to the station had been a bad idea. She'd known it before she'd gotten in the car. But that was the sort of stupid, irrational behavior she couldn't seem to control. Even though she'd never made it out of her car. Thanks to Evan Gann. People didn't know how to mind their own damn business.

If she'd gotten into the studio, she might have learned whether another settlement was being considered. The last offer the group had made, Rick had flatly refused. Although since she'd pumped Zach Hass, the new guy, for information, everyone named in the lawsuit had probably been warned not to talk to her. For all she knew, security wouldn't even have let her inside. Unless…

She abruptly brought her head up.

Evan Gann. He could get her inside. No one could stop her if she was going to see him. Dammit. Why hadn't she taken his number? Grudgingly, she pushed to her feet and got her cell phone. She hoped like hell his number was listed.

* * * * *

SPECIAL EDITION

Life, Love and Family

*These contemporary romances will strike a chord
with you as heroines juggle life
and relationships on their way to true love.*

New York Times *bestselling author*
Linda Lael Miller
*brings you a BRAND-NEW contemporary story
featuring her fan-favorite McKettrick family.*

Meg McKettrick is surprised to be reunited
with her high school flame, Brad O'Ballivan.
After enjoying a career as a country-and-
western singer, Brad aches for a home and
family…and seeing Meg again makes him
realize he still loves her. But their pride man-
ages to interfere with love…until an unex-
pected matchmaker gets involved.

*Turn the page for a sneak preview of
THE McKETTRICK WAY by Linda Lael Miller.
On sale November 20, wherever books are sold.*

Brad shoved the truck into gear and drove to the bottom of the hill, where the road forked. Turn left, and he'd be home in five minutes. Turn right, and he was headed for Indian Rock.

He had no damn business going to Indian Rock.

He had nothing to say to Meg McKettrick, and if he never set eyes on the woman again, it would be two weeks too soon.

He turned right.

He couldn't have said why.

He just drove straight to the Dixie Dog Drive-In.

Back in the day, he and Meg used to meet at the Dixie Dog, by tacit agreement, when either of them had been away. It had been some kind of universe thing, purely intuitive.

Passing familiar landmarks, Brad told himself he ought to turn around. The old days were gone. Things had ended badly between him and Meg anyhow, and she wasn't going to be at the Dixie Dog.

He kept driving.

He rounded a bend, and there was the Dixie Dog. Its big neon sign, a giant hot dog, was all lit up and going through its corny sequence—first it was covered in red squiggles of light, meant to suggest ketchup, and then yellow, for mustard.

Brad pulled into one of the slots next to a speaker, rolled down the truck window and ordered.

A girl roller-skated out with the order about five minutes later.

When she wheeled up to the driver's window, smiling, her eyes went wide with recognition, and she dropped the tray with a clatter.

Silently Brad swore. Damn if he hadn't forgotten he was a famous country singer.

The girl, a skinny thing wearing too much eye makeup, immediately started to cry. "I'm sorry!" she sobbed, squatting to gather up the mess.

"It's okay," Brad answered quietly, leaning to look down at her, catching a glimpse of her plastic name tag. "It's okay, Mandy. No harm done."

"I'll get you another dog and a shake right away, Mr. O'Ballivan!"

"Mandy?"

She stared up at him pitifully, sniffling. Thanks to the copious tears, most of the goop on her eyes had slid south. "Yes?"

"When you go back inside, could you not mention seeing me?"

"But you're Brad O'Ballivan!"

"Yeah," he answered, suppressing a sigh. "I know."

She rolled a little closer. "You wouldn't happen to have a picture you could autograph for me, would you?"

"Not with me," Brad answered.

"You could sign this napkin, though," Mandy said. "It's only got a little chocolate on the corner."

Brad took the paper napkin and her order pen, and scrawled his name. Handed both items back through the window.

She turned and whizzed back toward the side entrance to the Dixie Dog.

Brad waited, marveling that he hadn't considered incidents like this one before he'd decided to come back home. In retrospect, it seemed shortsighted, to say the least, but the truth was, he'd expected to be— Brad O'Ballivan.

Presently Mandy skated back out again, and this time she managed to hold on to the tray.

"I didn't tell a soul!" she whispered. "But Heather and Darlene *both* asked me why my mascara was all smeared." Efficiently she hooked the tray onto the bottom edge of the window.

Brad extended payment, but Mandy shook her head.

"The boss said it's on the house, since I dumped your first order on the ground."

He smiled. "Okay, then. Thanks."

Mandy retreated, and Brad was just reaching for the food when a bright red Blazer whipped into the space beside his. The driver's door sprang open, crashing into the metal speaker, and somebody got out in a hurry.

Something quickened inside Brad.

And in the next moment Meg McKettrick was standing practically on his running board, her blue eyes blazing.

Brad grinned. "I guess you're not over me after all," he said.

ATHENA FORCE

Heart-pounding romance and thrilling adventure.

She's their ace in the hole.

Posing as a glamorous high roller, Bethany James, a professional gambler and sometimes government agent, uncovers a mob boss's deadly secrets…and the ugly sins from his past. But when a daredevil with a tantalizing drawl calls her bluff, the stakes—and her heart rate—become much, much higher. Beth can't help but wonder: Have the cards been finally stacked against her?

ATHENA FORCE

Will the women of Athena unravel Arachne's powerful web of blackmail and death…or succumb to their enemies' deadly secrets?

Look for

STACKED DECK

by *Terry Watkins*.

REQUEST YOUR FREE BOOKS!

2 FREE NOVELS PLUS 2 FREE GIFTS!

HARLEQUIN®

Blaze

Red-hot reads!

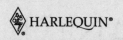

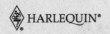

HARLEQUIN®

Blaze™

COMING NEXT MONTH

#363 A BLAZING LITTLE CHRISTMAS Jacquie D'Alessandro, Joanne Rock, Kathleen O'Reilly
A sizzling Christmas anthology
When a freak snowstorm strands three couples at the Timberline Lodge for the holidays, anything is possible...including incredible sex! Cozy up to these sizzling Christmas stories that prove that a "blazing ever after" is the best gift of all....

#364 STROKES OF MIDNIGHT Hope Tarr
The Wrong Bed
When author Becky Stone's horoscope predicted that the New Year would bring her great things, she never expected the first thing she'd experience would be *a great one-night stand!* Or that her New Year's fling would last the whole year through....

#365 TALKING IN YOUR SLEEP... Samantha Hunter
It's almost Christmas and all Rafe Moore can hear...is sexy whispering right in his ear. Next-door neighbor Joy Clarke is talking in her sleep and it's keeping Rafe up at night. Rafe's ready to explore her whispered desires. Problem is, in the light of day, Joy doesn't recall a thing!

#366 BABY, IT'S COLD OUTSIDE Cathy Yardley
And that's why Colin Reeves and Emily Stanfield head indoors—then it's sparks, sensual heat and hot times ahead! But will their private holiday hometown reunion last longer than forty-eight delicious hours in bed?

#367 THE BIG HEAT Jennifer LaBrecque
Big, Bad Bounty Hunters, Bk. 2
When Cade Stone agreed to keep an eye on smart-mouthed Sunny Templeton, he figured it wouldn't be too hard. After all, all she'd done was try to take out a politician. Who wouldn't do the same thing? Cade knew she wasn't a threat to jump bail. Too bad he hadn't counted on her wanting to jump him....

#368 WHAT SHE *REALLY* WANTS FOR CHRISTMAS Debbi Rawlins
Million Dollar Secrets, Bk. 6
Liza Skinner, lottery winner wannabe, *thinks* she knows the kind of guy she should be with, but is she ever wrong! Dr. Evan Gann is just the one to show her that a buttoned-down type can have a wild side and still come through for her when she needs him most....

www.eHarlequin.com

HBCNM1107